A DAMNED HARD WAY TO DIE

Dayne flopped onto the couch, grabbed the remote, and flipped through the TV channels. There was nothing but news on. "What the hell—" She saw something football-like flash onto the screen.

The Duke Blue Devils and the UNC Tarheels were on the field, and the Tarheel quarterback threw a beautiful long bomb down the field—and some huge guy in an obscene bright-red devil suit, with a pitchfork, no less, appeared out of nowhere and speared the football out of mid-air.

There was a cut to an anchorman who stood panting in front of the camera, his usually perfect hair mussed and his tie crooked. "All across the state, we have similar reports. We take you to the Ashboro Fan Faire where two deaths have been confirmed."

A reporter appeared, her face set in the fake-grim expression TV reporters always seemed to wear. "The final event of the Fan Faire ended in tragedy today when two filk singers performing 'I Wanna Be Seduced' were set upon by a bevy of what seemed to be nude women who attempted to seduce them on stage. Klingon security officers and men and women in Star Fleet uniforms acted quickly to restore order, but it was too late. The women turned out to be neither injured . . . nor women. In this interview, taped earlier, I talk with one, who claims she is a succubus straight from Hell."

Also by Holly Lisle

Fire in the Mist
Bones of the Past
Mind of the Magic

Minerva Wakes
When the Bough Breaks
with Mercedes Lackey
The Rose Sea
with S.M. Stirling
Mall, Mayhem & Magic
with Chris Guin

SYMPATHY FOR THE DEVIL

HOLLY LISLE

SYMPATHY FOR THE DEVIL

Copyright © 1996 by Holly Lisle

A Baen Books Original

Baen Publishing Enterprises
P.O. Box 1403
Riverdale, NY 10471

ISBN: 0-671-87703-8

Cover art by Clyde Caldwell

First printing, January 1996

Distributed by Simon & Schuster
1230 Avenue of the Americas
New York, NY 10020

Printed in the United States of America

Dedication

For Mark Twain and C.S. Lewis, who introduced me to this territory when I was nine; and in memory of Cathy Kelchner, my long-time friend, who lived long enough to see this project, but not to its completion. I miss you, Cathy.

Acknowledgements

Special thanks to my friends,
Bill Mullis and Keith Brinegar, who
were willing to die for the cause; and to
Bill Cleveland, Kerri Walters,
Cathy Lovato, and Walter Spence,
whose shrewd insights and wonderful
critiques changed the direction of the
book and made it infinitely better
than it was.

How can Hell exist if there is a Heaven,
or Heaven if there is a Hell?

Chapter 1

Lucifer—Puissant Lord of Evil, Utmost Originator of All Things Foul, Master of the Netherworlds, Purveyor of Anguish—glanced up from his newspaper to stare thoughtfully over the miles of open office space that made up the central nervous system of Hell. Uncounted thousands of imps and leccubi and damnedsouls sat at uncounted thousands of obsolete, cantankerous computer terminals, alternately typing and swearing. The air-conditioning was on the fritz again, and Hell's computers worked poorly in the resulting heat.

Lucifer's main office manager, the fallen angel Sertapius, had sent in a request for more computer techs. Unless things improved, he wasn't going to get them. They were hard to corrupt. They liked their work too much, and happy people didn't go to Hell. Lucifer had some of his top people working on a way to convince computer techs to get involved in politics—after all, bureaucrats were easy. Hell was up to the tips of its horns in them.

The news was about average—wars, famines, plagues, shootings, hatred, racism, sexism, politically correct fanaticism—in other words, all good. Lucifer flipped to the entertainment section and read *Calvin and Hobbes*,

1

which he enjoyed when Calvin was being terrible. And then he read his weekend horoscope—he always read his horoscopes. Some of his best future denizens wrote them, and he liked to check out the talent.

LIBRA—FELLOW LIBRAN, CONCERNED BY ISSUE OF FAIRNESS—LIKE ALL BORN UNDER YOUR SIGN—INTERCEDES ON YOUR BEHALF. BEGINNING OF NEW WEEK BRINGS YOU UNIMAGINED OPPORTUNITIES.

Lucifer arched an eyebrow and rubbed thoughtfully at the base of one of the curled ram horns that sprouted from his forehead. Promises, promises—the horoscopes were always full of them. Of course, where he was, nothing ever came of those promises.

That was the hell of Hell.

Chapter 2

Dayne Kuttner was trying to catch up on her charting. She kept one eye on the monitors—rows of green light slid across the black screens in a variety of ugly, irregular patterns. Nobody looked good today, and she waited tensely for the next lethal change.

She glanced at her watch and wrote: "1432. Systems assessment—see previous notes. Changes are as follows—both pupils now fully blown, no reaction to light. Sclerae edematous. Eyes lubricated, padded and taped. Decerebrate posturing noted . . ." She went through the list, noting every sign that the woman in bed 432-D wasn't going to be getting better. Mrs. Paulley, seventy-eight years old, had fallen down her stairs at home and fractured her skull. By the time her daughter had found her and gotten an ambulance, the old woman's brain had undergone irreversible damage caused by the swelling.

Her doctor was a huge believer in heroic measures, however. The old woman, at death's door, was given infusions to reduce the swelling inside her head, other infusions to regulate her erratic heart, further infusions to control her blood pressure—and then she'd been shipped upstairs to the ICU and Dayne.

And there she'd languished for over a week. When her breathing stopped, Dr. Batskold put her on a

3

ventilator. When her kidneys failed, he had the portable
dialysis unit brought in and he'd flushed her blood through
a machine.

She was in a coma. She was never going to see anyone
again, she was never going to sit up again or laugh again
or even breathe on her own again. She was never going
to be a human being again, and yet the ICU nurses
had orders to treat her as a full code—to take every
possible measure to keep her alive, no matter what that
measure was.

Dayne had protested this to Dr. Batskold after the
first dialysis.

"We're here to save them, Dayne," he'd said. It was
his perpetual response to Dayne's protests against what
she saw as his excessive heroics. He shook his head
and looked over at her—gave her his famous, kindly,
grandfatherly smile. "I don't play to lose, Dayne."

"It's my job as this patient's advocate to suggest that
what we are doing to her isn't in her best interests,"
Dayne told him.

Batskold raised an eyebrow. "Did you get a promotion?
I didn't hear."

"Promotion?"

"Promotion . . . to patient advocate. How exciting for
you." He'd looked down at Mrs. Paulley's chart. "I must
see a copy of your new job description."

"Every nurse is a patient advocate," Dayne had told
him.

He'd finished his orders and slammed the cover shut
on the chart. "Then why doesn't every nurse give me
the kind of trouble you give me, Dayne? No. You're
out of line here—overstepping your bounds. It's my
job to decide when we keep on trying. It's your job to
keep on trying. When God is ready for Mrs. Paulley,
He'll take her."

Dayne would have mentioned that God had been

trying to take Mrs. Paulley for over a week, but it wouldn't have done any good. Batskold's response to that was invariably, "He isn't trying hard enough then, is he?"

The conversation, days later, still ran through her head. She kept writing, angry. Sooner or later someone would review one of Batskold's charts and question his treatment of people who had no hope. They would look at the costs he was running up for families who would never be able to pay off the hundreds of thousands of dollars their bill would run; they'd look at the pain he was causing to those same people, by letting them hope for miracles that weren't going to happen; and someday, someone in authority would do something.

In the meantime, Dayne could do nothing more than she was already doing. Write down everything, question questionable orders . . . get written up by Batskold.

Out of the corner of her eye, she caught a change in the flickering pattern of light that scrolled across the monitor. The reading was Mrs. Paulley's, and it was bad. A run of PVCs—premature ventricular contractions. The ventricles of Mrs. Paulley's heart were pumping irregularly, a sign that could indicate they were going to quit pumping altogether at any time.

Dayne put the chart down and headed into the glass-walled room in front of her desk. She had certain things she could do without notifying Dr. Batskold, and she did them. She increased the amount of the cardiac medication that was running into Mrs. Paulley's veins, she brought in the crash cart, with its heart defibrillator and drawers full of emergency medications, and she checked to make sure Mrs. Paulley's IVs were still putting their medication into her bloodstream where it needed to be, and that they hadn't worked loose to pour it into her flesh, or into the bed. She checked to make sure the ventilator was working correctly, and that the tube carrying oxygen into the old woman's lungs was clear. She slipped a blood pressure cuff around the old woman's arm and checked her pressure—it had dropped.

Dayne looked at the over-bed monitor. She was starting to get regular runs of those same PVCs. She waved at the ward secretary. "Stacy! Page Dr. Batskold up here. I need him to take a look at this." Stacy nodded and got on the phone.

Dayne increased the dose of the cardiac medication again, and looked at the old lady lying in the bed, tiny, frail, pale and bruised, with bandages around her head and bandages over her eyes, with a huge white plastic tube shoved down her throat and Teflon catheters shoved into the veins of her neck. The ventilator hissed and chugged, forcing her chest up and down, the IVs clicked and beeped, the monitor ticked overhead.

Dayne walked over to the side of the bed and took the old woman's hand. Sometimes she sang to her comatose patients while she worked on them—hearing was supposed to be the last sense to go, and she wanted them to know someone was there, someone who still remembered they were human—but she didn't feel much like singing at that moment. Instead, she just talked.

"It's a pretty October day out there, Mrs. Paulley. The leaves are starting to turn, and the sky is so blue you'd think it was in a painting instead of real. Out your window I can see a mother and two little boys sitting on the bench over by the pond. They're feeding the ducks and a couple of Canada geese—throwing bread to them. The littlest boy is sitting on his mother's lap because one of the geese came right up to him and it was as big as he is."

She was watching the monitor—no improvement. She let go of the old lady's rigid hand and pulled a pre-filled syringe of the cardiac drug out of the cart. She injected it into the IV, wrote down the time she'd given the drug and the amount she gave on a paper towel, and watched for any change in that thin green line.

She said, "Your daughter called to tell me she and your two grandchildren would be stopping by this evening. You have a very nice family. They love you very much."

The ventilator hissed, the IVs dripped and beeped, and Mrs. Paulley's cardiac rhythm got worse. Dayne put the blood pressure cuff on automatic and set it to do a check every minute, then lowered the head of the bed until it was flat.

"Stacy," she yelled, "get the nursing supervisor and the respiratory therapist up here stat, and change Dr. Batskold's page to stat, too. She's going to code on me!"

Mary Deiner ran into the room. She was one of the other three RNs in the unit; her patients were bad, too, but the ICU nurses helped with each other's codes. "What do you want me to do?"

"Defibrillate when we need it. Push drugs. I'll do CPR."

Mary nodded, and warmed up the defibrillator. The high-pitched whine of that machine joined the rest of the machine noises in the cramped room.

Stacy came in and grabbed the code log. "Should I start it now?"

Dayne was running in a second bolus dose of the cardiac drug. "Not yet. She still has a viable rhythm." She shook her head. "No—go ahead and write these down." She handed the ward secretary the paper towel with the blood pressure and the two boluses of cardiac drugs noted, as well as the changes in the titration of the IV drips.

The blood pressure monitor showed that Mrs. Paulley's pressure had dropped. Her heart was failing fast in spite of everything Dayne tried.

"Increase the dose on her Nipride for me, Mary." The machine that ran the blood pressure medicine was closer to Mary than to Dayne.

Dayne studied the monitor. The wide, slashing Vs of the irregular ventricular beats still ran across the screen in clumps. Then all the normal beats vanished. The monitor showed nothing but a broad band of up-and-down slashes—its alarm went off at the desk with a scream. The blood pressure monitor alarmed at the same instant.

The old woman's heart was no longer moving blood through her lungs into her brain or other vital organs. She had no blood pressure and no pulse.

"Shock her," Dayne said to Mary. "Start at a hundred joules." That was a low amount of electricity, but the old woman was nothing but bones.

The supervisor and the respiratory therapist ran in as Mary pulled Mrs. Paulley's gown up and put the cold metal paddles on her chest. "Clear!" Mary yelled, and everyone stood away from the bed. There was a *whump* as the paddles discharged their electricity, then Dayne felt for a pulse at the woman's neck while she watched the monitor. The line that crawled across the screen was ragged and smaller, with no sign of a rhythm. Dayne found no pulse. "Nothing. She's in V-fib now. Give her a dose of epi, and if that doesn't work, we're going to shock her at two hundred."

Mary injected a drug that sometimes caused the heart to restart. It didn't work this time, though, and she warmed up the paddles to a higher voltage. "Clear!" she yelled, and again everyone stood back.

"Why are we doing this, Dayne?" the supervisor asked. "She's decerebrate."

"Her pupils are blown, too," Dayne said. "But she's Batskold's. He made her a full code—we're to do everything we can."

"Speak of the devil," the respiratory therapist said, as the doctor walked into the room.

"Where are we on this?" he asked.

Dayne gave him a quick rundown of all the steps she'd taken, ending with the summation that the old woman had not responded to anything.

"Shock at three hundred joules," he told Mary.

The paddles *whumped* again, and the room filled with the unmistakable odor of burned flesh. The old woman's heart rhythm remained absent.

"Start CPR."

Dayne climbed onto the edge of the bed, locked her hands together with her fingers raised and her right hand over her left, and began pressing into Mrs. Paulley's sternum with the heel of her left hand. "One-one-thousand, two-one-thousand, three . . ."

Everyone in the room heard the crunch as Mrs. Paulley's sternum cracked and her ribs broke. Dayne shuddered. Dr. Batskold said, "Keep going. If she lives, we can heal the ribs. We can't do anything for her if she's dead."

Dayne kept on compressing, forcing blood through the old woman's body. The ribs crunched beneath her hands with every push—a sound and a sensation she would relive in her nightmares. Meanwhile, Dr. Batskold pumped his patient full of drugs, tested the amount of oxygen in her blood, tinkering with the titrations of the drips he'd put her on. . . .

"There! You see?" he suddenly yelled. "We have a rhythm! Stop CPR!"

Dayne pulled back and automatically felt for a pulse. A thready one slipped beneath her fingers—but it was definitely there. Poor old woman.

"We won!" Dr. Batskold said, and grinned cheerfully around the room. "Good work, everyone. Okay—Dayne, standard orders. Let's get a chest X-ray and hourly ABGs and . . ." He rattled off a long list of orders, which Dayne wrote on the chart.

"Code status?" Dayne asked when he'd finished.

"Oh, definitely let's keep her a full code. Definitely. We don't concede defeat until we have to." He turned and, whistling, walked to the nurses' station to begin charting the annals of another of his victories over death.

"We *won*?" the nursing supervisor asked with a lift of her eyebrow. She stared at the comatose body in the bed.

"Oh, yeah," Dayne said softly. "Dr. Bastard always plays to win."

Chapter 3

Agonostis, Chief Fallen Angel in Charge of Lust and Fornication, buried his head in his hands and groaned. The quarterly numbers were in, and they were bad. Very, very bad.

Lust was still running well, but any idiot could sell lust—and he knew it, and he knew Lucifer knew it. Fornication was down, though. Adultery had dropped off a point and a third in the last quarter, down another point from the quarter before. If this continued, he was going to be hanging in his own little solitary space over the Infinite Nothing, like the lowliest of damned souls.

Diseases, he thought darkly. His problems were all because of diseases. Morality was no better than it had ever been—in fact, in many places and many ways, it was worse. But Jezerael, Chief Fallen Angel in Charge of Plagues, Illnesses and Social Diseases had gotten in good with the Big Guy, and had wangled out double the funding Agonostis had received on her research grants every year for the past fifteen years. And the daughter of a motherless pissant had spent every damned solidus on communicable diseases. Plotting, damn her eyes. She'd had this all figured out fifteen years ago— Agonostis would bet every soul in his laboratory on it.

Now Earth had untreatable tuberculosis, virulent

syphilis, AIDS, and herpes simplex type II. Everything was becoming resistant to penicillin—Agonostis' one-time favorite drug, since it made fornication so safe—and other drugs were becoming less effective, too. And even if he got those problems licked—and his lab techs were working as fast as they could to beat every single one of Jezerael's diseases—Agonostis figured his archenemy probably had new strains of Black Plague and typhoid waiting in the wings.

Agonostis had worked the condom angle as hard as he could, but people were getting smarter. They were realizing that condoms broke or slipped at inopportune times, or were defective—and they were starting to abstain.

Business was looking bad. And fornication used to be such a fun line of work.

What I need, he thought, is a miracle.

Unfortunately, miracles were hard to come by in Hell.

Chapter 4

Pitchblende, Lucifer's executive secretary, placed the most recent marketing reports on the Archfiend's glossy lacquered red desk.

Lucifer glanced through the hefty sheaf of papers—Vice, Usury, War, Disease, Famine, Telephone Solicitation . . . all the big evils were there.

The *Lust and Fornication American Quarterly* report showed good movement in the Lust Department. Miniskirts and see-through blouses were back in, sexual harassment suits were on the rise, and Agonostis had opened some very clever new markets by taking advantage of cutting-edge technology—pornographic CD-ROMs, computer sex-games, and online sex services were skyrocketing. Agonostis' R&D people were doing wonders with virtual reality technology, too, and expected to have their full-sensory-stimulus products on the market even before any practical VR applications became available.

Lucifer frowned when he saw the Fornication numbers, though. Fornication had been *the* blue-chip market since time began—an absolute sure thing guaranteed to produce steadily increasing revenues no matter what else was going on in the world. As long as there were more people (and there were always more people) fornication kept right on increasing. Yet

Agonostis' numbers were down—markedly down. If Lucifer remembered correctly, they had trended downward in the past two quarters as well.

The Archfiend tapped a few keys on his keyboard to bring up Quick'N'Dead, Hell's soul-accounting program, then ran through the graphs for Fornication for the last year, then the last three years, and finally the last five. He grew angrier with every new set of graphs. He should have checked this earlier—Agonostis had managed to counterbalance his Fornication numbers with his Lust numbers so that his reports still showed a net damnedsoul increase, but Lucifer discovered Fornication had been dropping off in fits and starts for five straight years. A five-year drop in a blue-chip asset could only come from poor management.

It was about time to remind Agonostis that not all jobs in Hell were desk jobs.

Lucifer nibbled on one long, pointed talon and contemplated risky, difficult field assignments.

Agonostis needed one.

Chapter 5

Dayne stripped out of her scrubs and threw them in a pile on the floor. She fished through the dryer and found a T-shirt, a pair of shorts and a pair of thick socks; she tugged those on angrily, then stormed around until she managed to locate her sneakers. She didn't pet either of the cats that twined around her ankles hoping for attention. She didn't check the messages on her answering machine, though the blinking light indicated that there were four— more than usual.

She ran up the stairs two at a time to the second floor of her two-story apartment, into the spare bedroom that she used as a gym, and moved the setting on her stair-stepper up to FAST.

She was furious—angrier than she had ever been. She was angry with Dr. Batskold, with herself, with the universe in general. She climbed on the stair-stepper, checked her watch, and started off at a running pace.

Mrs. Paulley had died twice more on the same shift. Both times, Dr. Batskold managed to get her back, and both times he gloated as if he'd done something wonderful.

Dayne's other patient, a young man who'd tried to kill himself with household chemicals and who didn't have any kidneys anymore, had gone into withdrawal from the other drugs he apparently had been taking without anyone knowing. She didn't even want to think about what she'd had to do to him. He'd sobbed and cried and begged her to just let him die—and she'd kept right on working on him, because it was her job, because she was a nurse and that was what nurses did. The Nazis had used the same excuse when questioned—they'd been following orders.

"Just like me. I feel like a damned Nazi. No I don't— I feel like Hell's chief torturer," Dayne snarled, pumping on the stair-stepper. She ran upstairs for twenty minutes, as fast as she could push the machine, then jumped off, sweating and breathing hard, and dropped to the floor. She did a hundred push-ups military-style, rested a moment, did a hundred more, rested a moment, and did a third set. She got up and settled onto the Roman chair, and did Roman chair sit-ups, two hundred and fifty at a time.

It didn't help. The anger still burned in her belly, hot and steady and real. She wasn't just angry about the things that had happened that day; the torture she'd put her patients through had wakened that other, older anger. And as mad as Dayne was at Batskold, she was madder at God. She blew through bench presses and flyes and lat pulldowns and rows and squats, pushing herself harder and harder, trying to take herself to a place beyond the anger—but there was no place inside her that the anger didn't touch.

She put the weights down at last and stood in the center of the room, breathing hard, and she faced the fears that ate at her.

More than once, she'd looked at herself as a torturer— as the person who did terrible things to nice little old ladies and to sweet old men, to people who were helpless and hopeless. She was only half joking when, talking with friends, she referred to her job as the job from Hell. One thing kept her in nursing—the fact that sometimes the terrible things she did to her patients made them better. Sometimes she was able to make things right.

But Dayne believed in Hell—in a real, literal Hell where the souls of the damned went to be tormented for eternity. She believed in Heaven, too, but thoughts of Heaven hadn't given her much solace in the four years since her husband Torry died.

She'd loved him. He drank, he ran around on her, he got into trouble, he was a failure as a husband and as a human being—but for the whole three years they were married, she'd loved him.

He died the way he'd lived—driving fast, stone drunk, with a woman who was not his wife in the car with him. He'd smashed into a telephone pole going at better than a hundred miles an hour, and he and his most recent girlfriend had flashed out of existence before they'd had a chance to know what happened to them.

And right now, Dayne thought, down in Hell, someone was torturing Torry.

She stood in the center of that room, thinking of the pain she inflicted—and the fact that she inflicted it as gently and quickly as she could, and of the fact that it ended—that no matter how badly she hurt the people she cared for, their pain ended. Dr. Batskold couldn't make them live forever, even though he tried. Sooner or later they would die and escape.

Torry couldn't escape. And when the universe blew out of existence and all of Time came to an end, someone would still be torturing Torry.

He'd been twenty-four when he died—young and beautiful and foolish. His fundamentalist parents had jammed religion down his throat until he'd thrown it up; he'd come to despise churches and religion and everything he connected with them, and his life had been one big attempt to spit in God's eye. Dayne had loved him anyway—not wisely, but with her whole heart.

In spite of everything, she still loved him—and for four years, she'd gotten up every morning and gone to bed every night, thinking of Torry in Hell.

This day, this hellish day that had come hard on the heels of a week of hellish days, had brought thoughts of Torry to the front of her mind, and heated up her anger until she couldn't hold it in anymore.

She looked up toward Heaven, and with her eyes wide open, she said, "Okay, God. I've had it. I've thought about this until I can't stand to think about it anymore, and now we're going to have to do something about it. You said that whatever we asked of you, if we had faith, you would give to us." She took a deep breath, and her hands clenched into fists.

"Hell is all wrong. You claim that we have free choice—the choice to love you or not, to follow you or not. But there isn't any choice to it. If a thief held a gun to my head and told me to give him my car keys or he'd kill me, I'd give him my keys . . . but nobody would say I did so of my own free will. And if he stuck the same gun to my head and told me to love him or else, I might pretend to love him . . . at least until I got hold of the gun.

"You're holding a gun to our heads, God. You're saying 'Love me or writhe in torment for eternity' and eternal torment is a pretty damned big gun for anything a person could do in eighty years.

"You claim to be a God of love. I say that only a sadistic, spoiled child would torture someone for eternity, no matter what reason he had."

She exhaled slowly, and her eyes narrowed. "You said ask and believe. So now I'm asking. Let them have the chance to repent, God. All of them. Every single soul in Hell. Let them have the chance to learn from the mistakes they made; let them into Heaven if they repent.

"Until you do this, you can consider me a conscientious objector, protesting the policies of Heaven. When I die, you can send me to Hell, because I won't go to Heaven until every soul can find a way there, God. Every soul. No matter who they were, no matter what they did.

"Eternity is too long for a loving God to condone the torture of his children."

Sweat ran down Dayne's face, mixing with her tears. She stood defiant, with her back straight and her head high, holding her own soul over the abyss, because her soul was the only thing she knew for sure God valued. She held her challenge up to God. She meant every word she said, with everything inside of her. And she believed.

Chapter 6

Klaxons blared, and the golden creature at the computer looked up from his work and said, "We have an incoming ten, your Holiness."

"A ten? Really? What was the last ten we received?"

"One Mary Beth Patterson, age eleven. Request for a horse." The angel grinned and shook his head ruefully.

"Of course. Request answered in a timely manner?"

"Absolutely, your Holiness."

"A horse." The Almighty Creator sighed.

The angel understood. Tens were requests asked in perfect purity and sincerity and belief, by people whose minds and souls were focused only on what they asked.

"Perhaps that was a poor example." The angel ran a quick search through Heaven's databases for all tens in the past five years, then brought the results up on the computer screen. The data scrolled out, glowing gold letters in a neat calligraphic hand on a background as richly black as infinite space.

> *Kerahatma Qrishi—age 7—request to spare mother's life—Granted*
>
> *Miguel Savarronda—age 9—job for father—Granted*
>
> *Caitlan O'Shaunessy—age 10 1/2—a border collie—Granted*

Brian Boucher—age 8—little brother healed of leukemia—Granted

Peter Derstman—age 9 1/2—principal punished for unfair punishment he gave—Granted

"That takes us through the last five years." The angel looked up at God and said, "I could run through the near-tens if you'd like. We have slightly more of those."

"No. That isn't necessary. My children ask with sincerity and pure hearts, and believe I will listen, and I always answer them, no matter how foolhardy their desires. What does this one want?"

The angel brought the newest request up on the screen.

Dayne Kuttner—age 28—God's sympathy for the devil, and second chance for the denizens of Hell—Status ... Pending.

"Good heavens," God murmured. "Is that a computer error?"

The angel typed in his query again, and the same data reappeared on the screen.

"Twenty-eight? She's really twenty-eight?"

"Yes, your Holiness." The angel started typing again.

"Let me see all tens through history, petitioners older than sixteen."

The angel nodded; he had already queried the computer for that information. In the thousands of years he had been record-keeper, he had gotten good at guessing what the Most Holy would ask for next.

Searching ...

"This may take a while."

It did take a while—Heaven had good computers, but unfortunately a lot of its information was stored in corollary sources which hadn't yet been added to the easy-retrieval databases. After a millisecond of real time—unconscionably slow by Heaven's clocks—the data started to come in. There was a ten from the first Buddha, one from an undiscovered saint in the Congo in the fifteenth century AD; there were the well-known tens from Moses and Peter, and of course a few from adults praying for the welfare of their children—the time and geographical distribution and religion of petitioner on those varied widely; and there was one from Abraham Lincoln. The angel remembered that one well. Preservation of the nation he loved—offered to pay whatever price was necessary if only his country could survive united.

There were others, too, but not many—thirty-seven all told since the first human had prayed to an unseen deity.

This one, the thirty-eighth in the entire history of humanity, was a humdinger. The angel had never seen anything even remotely like it.

"Bring up the full text as her soul phrased the request."

"You said ask and believe. So now I'm asking. Let them have the chance to repent, God. All of them. Every single soul in Hell. Let them have the chance to learn from the mistakes they made; let them into Heaven if they repent.

"Until you do this, you can consider me a conscientious objector, protesting the policies of Heaven. When I die, you can send me to Hell, because I won't go to Heaven until every soul can find a way there, God. Every soul. No matter who they were, no matter what they did.

"Eternity is too long for a loving God to condone the torture of his children."

The angel brought up a real-time picture of Dayne

as she prayed—she stared straight at them out of the monitor, her eyes flashing, her jaw clenched, her expression one of both purity and fierce determination.

"We never appreciate the requests for ponies and puppies when we have them, do we?" God mused. He pointed at the "Status . . . Pending" notation at the end of Dayne Kuttner's request, and sighed again, then chuckled. "She's a real firecracker, isn't she? Gave me an in-your-face chin-up challenge, too. I like that—no mealy-mouthed lukewarm bet-hedging there." God glanced over the angel's shoulder at the routing details appended to the request. "North Carolina, USA. And only a nominal Christian, though she certainly believes in me." The Almighty chuckled again. "I like to be sure of the ground rules before I act."

The angel cleared his throat. "Holy of Holies—the Fallen can be redeemed and released from Hell at any time if they only ask for forgiveness. So too can each and every damned soul. The Christian milieu is set up that way."

"I know that, but quite obviously Dayne Kuttner doesn't know that."

"If her request is granted even before she asks, what further action could possibly be necessary?"

God rested one hand on the angel's shoulder and said softly, "This young mortal has, in total seriousness, offered her soul up as a bartering piece to force me to give the Fallen a second chance. She doesn't know all the rules we operate by here, and she has no way of anticipating how I'll react. And yet, she believes with everything in her that I will listen, and she is using the only thing she knows for sure I value to make me care. That's no empty gesture. That's real love . . . a human who loves the worst and vilest of my sinners but hates the sin. I find that magnificent." God paused and tugged thoughtfully at his beard. He always wore a beard when he was in the Christian sector of Heaven—his Christian children expected one. "Not terribly well thought-out, perhaps, but magnificent.

"Hold her request in the buffer for me. I don't imagine we're going to get another ten in here any time soon, and I want to decide how to implement this. People who offer challenges to God should expect challenges themselves."

God laughed suddenly, and the angel shivered. God was known for his sense of humor; what few realized but the angel knew was that God was the first and perfect practical joker. And sure enough, God said, "Besides, this is a perfect opportunity to stir things up a little. A few Hellish paroles might make them think. The world has become far too complacent about me lately."

"You're granting her request then, your Glorious Holiness?"

"Of course I'm granting it. I always grant tens. It isn't as if I think Lucifer and his filthy hordes are going to come crawling on bended knee after all this time, anyway. But I reserve the right to implement tens as I see fit—and this one requires a careful study of the limitations I need to impose, and the benefits Heaven can gain from what will surely be perceived as a broad stroke. So just hang onto it. I'll be back to you when I've had a chance to work out the details."

The angel watched the Creator stalk away, head lowered in thought. Then he turned his attention back to the computer and deleted the "Pending" notice. He typed in the words, "Granted—implementation in progress."

Then he nibbled thoughtfully on his lower lip and stared off into the glorious infinity of heaven. He had a few dear friends who'd gotten involved on the wrong side of that first political disagreement—friends he hadn't seen in eons. With paroles on the way, he wondered if there might be some hope of getting back in touch.

Chapter 7

Friday night at nineteen hundred and thirty hours EDT on Hell's big clock, the imp on the soul radar yelped like an air raid siren and began bouncing around its station. It grabbed the mike and howled, "Holy Tarheels, Your Bat-Winged Arch-Fiendishness! Bogie on the big board! Bogie on the big board! And it's a whopper!"

Lucifer rose slowly from his work and stalked through the lined rows of desks, glowering, scattering secretaries with every step. When he walked, the rest of Hell went face down and shivered until the ground beneath it ceased to tremble with the passing of its lord. Flames curled up where Lucifer had stepped, and the stench of brimstone hung in his wake.

He reached the imp, and from his great and terrifying height, he looked down. Into the vast silence in the office, silence that came not of deference, but of dry-mouthed, unthinking fear, the Lord of Darkness growled, "What do you mean, doomed imp?"

The imp pointed to a swirling dot of white spinning against the deep red background of the soul-board. "Right there, O Foul Putrescence." The imp switched from doing Robin the Boy Wonder to doing Chuck Yeager. "Right smack in the heart of Charlotte, North Carolina—we got us a four-point-seven-nine plus-soul crosscurrent intersecting on the material plane with a triple-A hardcase bearing zero-zero-ninety and carrying an unidentified soul-cargo anomaly aimed straight at us, Roger Wilco, over and out."

"Little imp," Lucifer snarled, picking the imp up by the scruff of the neck, "tell me what you are called, that I may remember to curse you more fully after I have ground your very soulstuff into paste, ingested it, and shat it into the Bottomless Pit."

The imp squirmed and shook. "Er . . . Earwax, Your Hellishness."

"Earwax. You have only the time between one heartbeat and the next to tell me, *Earwax*, what exactly it was that you just said, or I will see that you spend an eon simply finding all your scattered atoms and pulling them back together before you can reform yourself into so much as a slime mold."

"Good-guy-upstairs-stirring-things-up-with-the-Big-Guy-and-looking-at-us," Earwax whimpered in one terrified breath, while he dangled thirty feet in the air from the Evil One's needle-tipped talons. "In Charlotte, North Carolina," it added.

"Charlotte, North Carolina, eh?" The Archfiend stared off into infinite space, thinking. "It seems to me we do a better than average business there . . . Oh, yes. *That* Charlotte. Automotive damnation cases—Hell's draftsmen designed the roads."

Lucifer realized he was still holding the imp; with a snort of disgust, he pitched it over his shoulder and it bounced four times, then scurried away. The Archfiend bent over the soul-radar and watched the bright swirls of energy that indicated the building fronts of good and evil—the pattern, a spiraling storm center that spun slowly around a central eye, would have looked at home on a hurricane tracking chart. It indicated building tension, the coming of a big event . . .

. . . And the Angel of Darkness knew that big events

always left plenty of wandering souls in their wake—souls that with minimal effort could be corralled into his domain.

He needed to get a team ready. He didn't know *what* was about to break—only God could tap directly into the lines of future events, but he could track their shadows and be ready.

And Agonostis—whatever was going to happen, this would be the perfect punishment for him. Agonostis didn't know it yet, but he was about to get a demotion.

Lucifer smiled slowly, and called up his list of servants who were furthest out of favor, and nearest to being downgraded to the unrank of damnedsouls and thrown into the Pit. These little special assignments always did much to stir up the enthusiasm of his deadweight employees. Sheer terror was a marvelous motivator.

Chapter 8

Dayne felt at peace. She stood in the shower with the icy water pounding on her back and smiled—it was as if God had lifted the weight of eternity off her shoulders. He'd heard her; and somehow she was sure he'd paid attention. She had never been so confident in her life that things were going to be okay—and although she didn't understand the feeling, she accepted it.

She stepped out of the shower to find Athos and Porthos sitting and watching.

She grinned. "Hi, guys." She bent down and scratched Athos behind the ears, dripping on him at the same time. The cat didn't mind, though Porthos would have stalked away with a wounded expression on his face had she tried the same trick with him. "Sorry I was in such a bad mood when I got home. I feel better now, though. So . . . you guys want something to eat?"

At the word "eat," both cats stood and Porthos yowled musically.

"Right. Silly question." She toweled off and pulled on a sleep shirt. She intended to spend the rest of the night sitting in front of the television, eating buttered popcorn and playing zombie. She had the next day off—her first day off in nine days, and she intended to sleep late, eat junk food, and otherwise make herself happy.

Chapter 9

God was chuckling as he strolled back to his secretary's desk.

"I've got it," he said. He handed the secretary a beautiful scroll and said, "Key this in and send it on the Hotline straight to Hell. Make sure it's perfect when you send it—I don't want those fiends finding any loopholes I didn't intend." He chuckled. "I expect they'll cause quite enough trouble making use of the few I did intend."

The angel unrolled the scroll and began to read. Its eyes went huge and round and it said, "Your Holiness . . . are you serious?"

"Oh, certainly. I haven't done any miracles in ages . . . they've been too busy doing miracles of their own. Space travel, television, electronics, medicine . . . they've been very busy. But I think a miracle they can't ignore and can't debunk will be a lot of fun."

"But don't you think this will give . . . er . . . *him* an edge?"

God rested a hand on the angel's shoulder and said, "Evil never has the edge it thinks it has. People will surprise you. They certainly surprise me, even now. No, I think this will shake loose some people who have been growing complacent. It will wake my children up." He chuckled again. "Besides, I haven't allowed myself the pleasure of seeing that miserable old goat dance to my tune in years. I think this is the sort of tune that will get him stepping, don't you?"

"Oh, yes," the angel said, staring at the long scroll covered with Lucifer's marching orders. "I certainly do."

Chapter 10

The fiery finger of doom seared a path down Agonostis' spine. He hurried down the circular stairway, swearing and snarling. The blazing summons in his hand left no doubt in his mind that he was in deep shit—he just hoped when he got the bad news he knew was coming, he wouldn't find himself literally so.

Eventually he reached the bottom of the stairs and swept through the arched stone doorway into a dimly lit hall whose roof seemed to reach to black infinity. That was the other thing that tipped him off. Lucifer gave promotions in the office. When he met one of his servants in the throne room, the news was invariably foul.

An onyx throne stood at the end of the long room, and the darkly beautiful figure of Agonostis' prince lounged there, waiting. Standing, Lucifer would have towered thirty feet tall. Even seated, he looked down on Agonostis, who, a single rank beneath the Archfiend, stood fifteen feet high himself.

Agonostis always felt his insides knot when facing his master.

"You're late, Agonostis."

"Yes, my lord." There was no way not to be late getting to the throne room—it could only be reached by walking down those steps, and the steps extended—and kept

extending—until the petitioner going down to face
Lucifer was exactly late enough to put the Archfiend
into a fine rage. Hell's architects had designed it that
way . . . and Agonostis hoped every one of them got a
chance to try the damned steps out, too.

Lucifer was holding the report—Agonostis couldn't
help but think of it as The Report.

"Your Fornication numbers have fallen off," the Prince
of Evil said in a cold, terrifying voice.

"There's a plague on—sexually transmitted diseases."
Agonostis winced at confessing that his problem was
one caused by his archrival. But he forged onward.
"Fornication fell off during the Black Plague, too. I've
kept the losses from becoming too severe by pushing
condom distribution in high schools and by making safe
sex a big, public topic, and I've made fornication a civil
rights issue instead of a moral issue, which I think was
very clever of me. Your Evilness, all of this will blow
over anyway as soon as my people come up with decent
vaccines for the diseases they're dealing with. And it
isn't like I'm behind on net—I've managed to offset
the losses in fornicators by increasing souls damned
by lust. My overall numbers are still up."

"Your Fornication numbers are *down*. Any idiot should
be able to maintain steady growth in that area of
damnation; humans have a natural inclination to damn
themselves in that direction anyway."

"I'd like to see any idiot try," Agonostis muttered.

"Would you really?" Lucifer smiled slowly, and
Agonostis instantly regretted the words. "Well, you'll
have the opportunity to do so. I'm demoting you to
field operative on a special away mission—meanwhile,
Jezerael will be promoted into your old post as Chief
Fallen Angel of Lust and Fornication. We'll see if she
can do a better job than you."

Agonostis hated field op work. But his ears caught

the second half of his new job description and his eyes narrowed. "*Away* mission? What the hell is an 'away mission'?"

Lucifer's smile grew broader. He pulled out a sheet of yellow paper and said, "I just got this off the Hellex. Straight from He Whose Name Shall Not Be Spoken, no less. Let me read it to you—I'm sure you'll find it enlightening."

The Archfiend read:

" 'Command from on High

" 'By order of the God of Heaven and Earth, Creator of All Things . . .' blah, blah—You know how he loves to tack on the titles when he's sending messages to us—"

" 'O fallen angel who is anathema to me, you whose name shall not pass my lips until you have humbled yourself before me—' "

Lucifer grinned. "Nice to know he's still smarting from that first dust-up. I'm looking forward to the next one. In any case—"

" 'By my order and on my express command and through the intercession of my daughter, Dayne Teresa Kuttner, you shall send forth out of Hell, under my parole, exactly fifty-eight thousand eight hundred fifty-one fallen angels, devils, demons, and assorted members of the lower orders of Hell's crawling vermin into the state of North Carolina—this number being exactly one one-hundredth of the human population in that state at the instant of my reckoning.

" 'Unchained denizens of Hell must obey the following rules:

❏ They will neither inflict, nor pay to have inflicted, any physical harm on any human.
❏ They will not parent a child with a human, either with or without the human's consent.
❏ They will not steal by supernatural means.
❏ They will not cause any disease or plague,

nor will they act as the agents through which any disease or plague is transmitted.

❑ They will not impersonate a minister, God, or angel of God, or any divine messenger of God.

❑ They will not cause any virgin births.

❑ They will not leave the State of North Carolina.

" 'The Unchained denizens of Hell may:

❑ Lie, tempt, deceive, mislead, and otherwise carry out the usual agenda of Hell.

❑ Impersonate human beings if that is within their nature and capacity.

❑ Own property, become citizens, hold offices, own and operate legal businesses, marry humans—if the humans are apprised of their true nature beforehand and no intimidation is used—and in all other legal ways approved by the State of North Carolina attempt to achieve a normal life on Earth.

❑ Enter into binding contracts with human beings—with one of the two following stipulations:

    1) The human must be fully apprised of the nature of the contract and the nature of all parties involved in the contract; or,

    2) The human must sign the contract with his own blood. (Percentage of blood to inert materials not specified; blood must be less than twenty-four hours old in Earth-sequential time *only*, as per previous agreements between Heaven and Hell; human must know that blood has been drawn; no blood from blood donorship or other merciful blood collection agencies,

or from accidents and injuries may be used.)

" 'Repent.'

"Repent," Lucifer muttered again, and cocked an eyebrow at Agonostis. "It is going to be the duty of my away commander to make sure there aren't any *repenters*." His voice was ominous when he said it. He continued to read:

" 'Unchained denizens of Hell must:

❏ Eat and drink mortal food, or their Earthly bodies will wither and fail, and they will have to pay Heaven for new ones. Heaven will charge a cost-per-body fee plus punitive wastage tax for any Earthly bodies above and beyond the one that will be issued free from Heaven per Hell-soul at the time of exit from Hell—this will be collected by the usual revenue methods. These Heaven-issued Earth-bodies will be indistinguishable from the individual Hellspawn's normal form and will have all the Hellspawn's usual abilities excluding those which would run counter to the above decrees.

❏ Obtain their sustenance in the normal mortal way—that is, by growing food or paying for it with cash or barter.' "

Agonostis swallowed. "And I am to be one of these Unchained, treading the Earth and seducing humans into damnation while . . . holding down a job?"

Lucifer laughed. It was a harsh and hollow sound. "Oh, I wouldn't think of demoting you as far as that . . . yet. No, no, Agonostis." The Archfiend looked down at Agonostis and his eyes blazed red. "You're going to be in charge. This will be your chance to prove to me that you still have what it takes to make it as a fallen angel in Hell. We haven't had one of the original Fallen

busted back to imp since ... gracious! ... since that
unfortunate incident with Shedhurdzashel and the failed
temptation of Billy Graham. You remember that, of
course."

Agonostis nodded. He was feeling faint.

"So I'm sure you'll come through for me."

"I'm going to be responsible for fifty-eight thousand
Hellspawn ..." Agonostis swallowed again. His heart
felt as if it was lodged in his throat. "On Earth. What
sort of tracking facilities will I have?"

"I'll finance a nice central office, and rent space
for several satellite offices—and make sure you're
supplied with start-up technology—"

"I'll probably rather buy locally," Agonostis said, thinking
of Hell's equipment, which was slightly more archaic than
Communist Russia's had been, and which was built and
tested by equally enthusiastic, inspired workers.

"—*technology*," Lucifer repeated stiffly, "an adequate
staff, some seed capital, and a base starting salary for
you and your officers. I'll expect net profits within the
fiscal year—we'll run it from October to October for
the sake of accounting convenience."

"You mean net profits in souls?"

"I mean net profits in souls *and* money. We're
incurring expenses from Heaven from this—I expect
to counterbalance those expenses and make a nice net,
too. If you're going to be on site, make it worth my
while to have you there."

Agonostis nodded. Keep fifty-eight thousand plus
Hellspawn in line with Hell's stinking equipment and
God's stinking rules *and* generate a profit. He'd known
this was going to be bad. He hadn't imagined the depths
to which bad could sink. "Yes, your Foulness," he said,
keeping his eyes on the ground. He sighed deeply and
turned to go.

"That isn't all, Agonostis."

Agonostis' skin began to itch—he knew the hives would be coming at any time. "Sir?" he said slowly.

"I want you to give the damnation of one particular mortal your special attention."

Agonostis didn't want to know, but he looked at his lord and master and asked, "Who, sir?"

The Archfiend's grin was especially evil as he said, "Dayne Teresa Kuttner, of course."

Agonostis would have wept if he could have. Those people who could request major favors from God—like the Unchaining of nearly sixty thousand Hellspawn, for example—and get God to answer were not people whose damnation he wanted to hear depended on him. He felt suddenly that he knew how Shedhurdzashel had felt when he'd been commanded to corrupt Billy Graham.

The Malevolent One patted him on the head. "I know how you would loathe being an imp, Agonostis. So don't let me down on this."

"No, Your Loathsomeness." Agonostis was remembering the imp he'd eaten earlier in the day for bringing his daily paperwork to him late. He didn't want to be an imp at all.

"Well, then. You'd best hurry. The rest of the away team is already packing—you're to leave in one hour. I'll expect you to stop by the main office on your way out to pick up a list of your orders and rules and my . . . suggestions. I'll expect you to find ways around God's rules, too."

"How are we to get . . . out?"

Lucifer shrugged. "God is providing the transportation on this. I have no idea what method he intends to use."

Agonostis nodded silently and turned away again, and again Lucifer stopped him. "There's no time limit on the rest of the assignment, but I want Dayne Kuttner's soul in my ledger in thirty days."

Agonostis' shoulders drooped. *Thirty days?* Without

a word, he left the throne room and climbed up the stairs, which stretched evilly on the way back up—simply because he was depressed—and returned to his office, still dragging.

Jezerael, swearing mightily, was throwing things out of Agonostis' desk when he got there. The other fallen angel glared up at him, and without a word, went back to flinging things that didn't belong to her across the cubicle.

Agonostis' spirits lightened. "Heard you got a promotion," he said.

Jezerael's swearing got louder.

"Heard you're going to get Fornication back on line." Agonostis chuckled. "Though with all those awful plagues Earthside, I'll be very interested to see how you do that." He clucked his tongue and shook his head in mock solicitude.

Jezerael threw an obscene gesture and said, "I heard *you* got a *de*motion."

Agonostis smiled at her. "Sixty thousand of Hell's finest doing my bidding, a main office and satellite branch offices, and a vacation someplace cool and green—I don't know that I'd call that a demotion."

"The grapevine . . ."

". . . Is full of sour grapes, Jezerael. You know that."

Agonostis picked up his belongings before Jezerael could break any more of them and strolled out of the office looking cheerful. He didn't allow his depression to show again until he was back in his quarters.

Then, however, he dropped into his wing-back chair and buried his head in his hands and muttered to himself.

"Keep all of Hell's little devils in line, Agonostis. Don't let them repent, Agonostis. Make money, Agonostis. Bring me Dayne Kuttner's soul, Agonostis. In one *month*, Agonostis. And she's going to take one look at me and kneel and clasp her hands and say, 'God, get that thing out of here,' and—Bam!—there I'll be. Agonostis the Grease Stain. Maybe I should just spit in Lucifer's face and let him turn me into an imp now."

He had one hour to get ready.

Less than one hour—the steps from Hell had eaten some of that time.

He sat up and stiffened his spine and took a deep breath.

"Agonostis," he told himself, "you've dragged more souls into Hell than any other Hellspawn in existence. You've dragged the mightiest and the purest through the mire, and you had fun doing it." He nodded sharply. "What you told Jezerael wasn't a lie. You've been made commander of your own army—almost sixty thousand strong, and surely the worst Hell has to offer." He grinned. "And you're operating with God's permission."

There was an American phrase that came to mind— shooting fish in a barrel. "That's it," he said. "This is shooting fish in a barrel. And as for Dayne Kuttner— well, Agonostis, you've never had the opportunity to go one-on-one with a single human soul before. Let's see how this woman stands up to the Lord of Lust."

He thought over the rules Lucifer had read to him, and when he considered them, he could think of dozens of ways to stay within the letter of the law while still completely subverting its spirit. Agonostis reached a decision. He stood and materialized himself into the Earthside operations computer room. He faced the mainframe that took up the central portion of the room and said in a loud voice, "Computer, I need a complete file on Dayne Teresa Kuttner and regional maps of the area in North Carolina that she inhabits with all the hot sin-spots marked out. Generate a database of our souls in the area, too, hard copy and disk media—I intend to set up a branch office wherever she lives. Also, I'll need the complete list of the troops assigned to me, and their specialties. Give me those in hard copy and disk, too."

The box hummed ominously, then subsided. The words, GO AWAY, YOU INCOMPETENT BOOB— I'M BUSY, scrolled down the screen.

Agonostis gritted his teeth. He said, "Tell me what I need to know or I'll have you reprogrammed by gargoyles."

The computer flashed a different message. YOU'RE IN HOT WATER WITH THE ARCHFIEND, SHITHEAD. DON'T THREATEN ME.

Agonostis bit the inside of his lip. God was going to suck him out of Hell and dump him somewhere on Earth in a very short time, and he didn't know who, or what, he was up against. "I want those records now."

YOU'LL WAIT UNTIL I FIND THEM.

"I'm not in *that* much trouble, Computer. Nor was I joking about the gargoyles." Agonostis pressed the palm of his hand against the side of the computer, and ran a short, sharp spike of power through the circuits. "If you try to screw with me, I'll melt your chips and your soul can come back as shit on the soles of the feet of the damned . . . and you can spend a millennia or two working your way up to gargoyle junior grade. Got that?"

The computer grumbled and snarled and growled. GOT IT.

"I thought you might. Give me the list of Unchained right now. Have an imp bring my materials to me in the anteroom in ten minutes, and immediately notify all lieutenants and above who are going to Earth to meet me there at the same time."

A disk and a sheaf of fireproof paper appeared in Agonostis' outstretched hand.

Agonostis dematerialized into a pocket of fast-time, set to exist for nine minutes. He set his own personal time for twenty-four hours, and in that twenty-four hours he set up his battle plans and made assignments and created well-focused disorder out of chaos. The energy drain on his soul required to compress time so fiercely and to hold it for so long was enormous, and he was literally sweating blood by the time he'd completed the plans. But he had them, and they were good.

He appeared in the anteroom to discover his command scurrying in the door and scrambling for seats; the room bustled with activity.

Agonostis cleared his throat, and the throng fell silent.

"All right, you. Hell is taking its business to Earth, and I am in charge. You make a mistake, you'll answer to me—and if you screw up badly enough, I'll make you wish you were still damnedsouls hanging in the Pit. Do . . . you . . . understand?"

"Yes, Lord Agonostis!" they shouted.

Agonostis nodded curtly. "Fine. These are your orders." He outlined the plan he'd worked out in slow-time.

Chapter 11

The light on her answering machine blinked incessantly. Dayne decided to listen to the messages before she made her popcorn. Five messages instead of the four that had been there when she got home. Somebody must have called while she was in the shower.

<beep> "Hey, Dayno. It's Greg. Lucy and I are going to be in town next weekend—I've got a project down your way and the company is flying us in. If you're going to be there, we'd love to stop by and see you. Give me a call back when you can."

Her oldest brother and his wife rarely made it down from Minnesota. Dayne was scheduled to work the entire next weekend, but might be able to swap some time with a couple of her colleagues; they owed her since she'd covered for them while they had the flu. She made a note to herself to call the hospital first thing the next morning to start lining things up.

<beep> . . . *<click>*

She hated hangups.

<beep> . . . *<click>*

Another one.

<beep> "I *hate* talking to these things. Geez, Dayne— are you *ever* going to get home? When you get off work, come over. Mike got a great deal on steaks and we need to use them up. Call before you come and we'll have

yours ready when you get here. Any time will be fine. We're going to be up late."

That was Paige, who never identified herself on the answering machine, and usually refused to leave messages. Most likely the two previous hang-ups had been hers. Dayne paused the machine and considered. Paige called when she wanted Dayne's company; she also called when she'd just met a single man she thought Dayne would like and had decided it was time to try matchmaking again. There was absolutely no way to tell which kind of call this was.

"So how much do I want a grilled steak?" she asked the cats.

They sat on the floor in the kitchen, watching her with inscrutable expressions.

"I don't know either."

She pushed the pause button.

<beep> .... *<inhale>* .... *<exhale>* .... *<inhale>* .... *<exhale>* .... *<inhale>* .... *<exhale>* .... "I'm watching you" .... *<inhale>* .... *<exhale>* .... *<click>*.

Her stomach twisted. The call had come while she was in the shower. Was it a coincidence? No one could see her in the shower, though maybe someone might have been able to see her in her spare bedroom working out. Had she left the blinds up? She'd been really angry when she was up there.

She shivered and stared at the goosebumps on her arms.

Most of the time, being alone was better than being married had been—but when she'd been married, she'd never gotten phone calls like that. As it was, she didn't get them often. They still felt ugly though.

The procedure the police had for dealing with such calls was complicated, and the phone company's was about equally so. She'd called both when she'd had a similar problem over a year earlier. She frowned and stared at her answering machine. There had to be something *she* could do to get rid of the caller . . . something she could say.

She sat down with a pencil and paper and made a few notes—things that would convince whoever was doing this to go away. She juggled her ideas back and forth, and finally came up with a message she liked. She practiced it a few times, letting her anger work through into her voice, then began recording.

"You have reached a number that is currently under surveillance," she said, pitching her voice low and mean. "Under FCC regulations and state and federal wiretapping and recording guidelines, I am required to inform you that all calls to this number are being recorded, and will be admissible as evidence in police procedures and in a court of law. Leaving a message implies informed consent. If you still wish to leave a message, do so after the beep."

She stopped the recording and grinned. Let the jerk think about *that* for a while.

The phone call decided her, though. She felt like having steak for dinner on somebody else's nickel, and more importantly, she felt like getting out of the house and going someplace where there were people. If Paige was trying to fix her up, maybe the guy would be someone interesting. If Paige was not trying to matchmake, Dayne would have the pleasure of visiting with friends for an evening instead of watching reruns.

And if the jerk called back, he'd get the machine.

She dialed Paige's number. "Paige . . . I'm on my way over—but don't let Mike throw the steak on the grill just yet. I think this time I want it still kicking a bit."

When she hung up, the thought that the person leaving the messages might actually be watching her recurred.

She considered options; she had the apartment about as burglar-proof as she could make it. There were deadbolts on both doors and all the windows were pinned—but she might need some security measures available to her when she answered the door. She was strong for her size, and fast—but she was also five-feet-nothing and she weighed ninety-seven pounds. She couldn't rely on strength. Instead, she'd have to rely on leverage—just like in nursing. Her eyes narrowed. Just like in everything, really.

She ran upstairs and rummaged around until she found both of her old baseball bats. She'd been on the hospital softball team for a couple of years, and had spent more than a little time practicing.

She rested one bat behind each door. That would do for a start.

She pulled a couple of spare canisters of pepper gas out of her kitchen junk drawer and put one of those near each door, too. Pepper gas was nasty stuff, better than mace or tear gas or ammonia-water or anything else she knew of for stopping attackers, either two- or four-legged. With her apartment armed, she found some jeans and a rugby shirt and her presentable sneakers, and jogged out the door with a third canister of pepper gas tucked inconspicuously into her front jeans pocket. She looked at her watch as she got into the car—nine P.M. already. Pretty late for dinner, she thought. She hoped Paige and Mike had been serious about staying up.

She was halfway to her destination when something big and red dashed across the road in front of her headlights. It was only where she could see it for an instant—far too short a time for her to identify whatever it had been. She slammed on the brakes, hoping to get a second glimpse . . . the thing had almost looked like someone in a costume, though it had had an animal's shambling, loose-limbed gait . . . but then the eerie feeling that she was being watched made her decide to hurry on.

She arrived at Paige's house still frowning, convinced that what she had seen was *wrong* somehow.

She wished she'd gotten a better look.

Chapter 12

The light had come while Agonostis was still finishing laying out his battle plans—without sound or warning, Heaven had taken Lucifer's hand-picked Hellspawn from whatever part of Hell they'd been in. Fifty-eight thousand eight hundred fifty-one damned vanished from the bowels of Hell. From the lowliest gargoyle and gremlin to the mightiest of fallen angels, they blinked out of existence in one location and blinked back into existence somewhere else.

But each of them was in a *different* somewhere else.

Agonostis looked around. He was alone, in the middle of somebody's garden, stark naked and in his original form. He had *not* intended to arrive in such a fashion. He'd been expected to stop by the office to pick up his final orders; he'd failed to do that, and the fact that it was God's fault wasn't going to cut any ice with the Father of Lies. Lucifer only cared about results, and the results he cared about were being screwed up because Agonostis hadn't followed orders.

Agonostis took a deep breath and nearly choked from the surprise—the air was clear, with a great deal of oxygen in it and neither sulfur nor brimstone. He stopped worrying about Lucifer for a moment and simply looked around. His night vision was very good—he could see a wealth of detail from the terrain around him on this nearly moonless night. The soft greens of grass, the rich reds and golds and yellows of leaves, the bright flowers in their matching hues of reds and oranges and golds, the cozy houses and gentle sounds and sweet smells overwhelmed him. The warm yellow light that spilled across neatly-mown grass seemed welcoming.

Unlike the lower orders of the Unchained, who had worked their way up from damnedsouls, and so had known only Earth and Hell, Agonostis had known Heaven before he was cast down—and if this place where he found himself was not Heaven, it was at least close.

He stretched—nothing hurt. He moved slowly. Still no pain. He jumped up and down vigorously, trampling huge holes in the garden—his body rejoiced in its vigor and its freedom from the constant throbbing agony of Hell.

He shouted—and a clear, icy, evil voice in his head said, "Do you intend to bounce naked on that dirt until your month is up and I recall you and turn you into an imp—or are you ready to get busy now?"

Agonostis froze. "God took us early, stripped our possessions from us, and scattered us," he said. "I have neither clothes nor supplies nor the money to buy them."

"*I—know—that.* You're fortunate you told your officers where to gather their troops; had you not done that, you would very likely have to round up every single one of the Hellspawn yourself. As it is, your inferiors, dreading your wrath, are out busily beating the bushes for you. And if you'll simply get yourself to Charlotte, I have your initial consignment of supplies waiting. I was going to leave you without them, but I decided I didn't want God to get the jump on us quite that quickly, since that was obviously his intent. I'd rather get even with him now . . . and you later."

Agonostis nodded. He shut his mind, effectively

blocking out Lucifer's voice, then concentrated on locating waiting supplies. Some of Hell's computers sat in the pile, their souls shifting and stretching as they tried to get a feel for the world in which they found themselves. He focused on those, and closed his eyes, and thought himself to them.

The supplies sat in an abandoned warehouse—computers and peripherals, racks of clothes and boxes of shoes, boxes and crates of things someone had thought might be necessary in bringing Hell to North Carolina. Agonostis found the manifest, slipped into slow-time, and checked it off—he had no intention of signing in blood without being certain every single item on the manifest actually existed. And as he reached the end, he was pleased with himself for having checked. The manifest noted that five million dollars accompanied the rest of the supplies—Lucifer's war chest was deep. But the actual amount of cash in the bags was only two and a half million.

"Where's the rest of the money?" Agonostis snarled into thin air.

"Oh, just cross through that amount and write in the correct amount and initial it," Lucifer said into his head.

"Not a chance. I'm not signing for anything until this manifest is correct."

"Oh, nonsense," the Archfiend said. "I'll send the other half along later."

"Now, or I don't sign. I'm not going to make myself responsible for repaying two point five million dollars I didn't even get. I won't do it."

"You become annoying quickly," Lucifer said, but the extra money appeared. Agonostis counted it, and on an impulse, checked serial numbers on the bills. About half of them were the same. "I won't do this—" he started again, but with a flash of ugly red fire and the stench of Hell, real money in the proper amount appeared.

He moved back into real time as the first of his officers appeared. "Devils, demons, and leccubi—clothes are here. Sludgewight," this to an ugly devil, even by Hell's standards, "you're paymaster until Squige reports in. Any variances in the accounts, I will personally take out of your hide." This was no empty threat. Agonostis had discovered several crates of Hell's most up-to-date torture implements. Since, by God's rules, he wasn't going to be able to use them on his human prey, he might as well get some good from them; they'd be ideal in keeping his underlings in line.

An imp appeared—a vibrant blue imp with enormous bat-wing ears and a face like a train wreck. "Mighty Lord Agonostis," he said in a shockingly deep, rich voice, "Earwax, here, reporting for duty."

Agonostis looked down at the imp and said, "I ate you for breakfast today, didn't I, imp?"

The imp's blue flesh paled to a dusty, near-white color, and the obnoxious creature went down on its knees. "No, Great and Terrible Lordship—I am not that imp. I am the imp Lucifer gave you as your personal aide and gofer."

Agonostis smelled something worse than rat in that setup. "He did, did he? And what did you do before this?" Agonostis reached out a finger and touched the imp's forehead, and the fiery power of Hell itself flickered between them. The little imp froze.

Mesmerized, it answered, and its voice was flat and hollow. "Insubordination, mostly. I fetched for Pusbucket as a low-level imp, operated a phone at central communications as a mid-level imp, and recently received a promotion—I read soul radar in the main office; and just today I made the Evil One angry at me. He gave me to you because he said you would eat me within a week, and then I would be out of the way . . . and he could charge you for the body."

Agonostis pondered. Earwax wasn't a spy, then. That was something to the good. He was likely to be a pain in the ass, and that wasn't good. Agonostis didn't feel like owing Lucifer for the body, though, so he determined that the imp's skin would stay intact—barring extraordinary circumstances. He would decide those as he went along.

Agonostis took the whammy off of him. "So you can answer a phone, can you?"

"Oh, yes, your Stupendously Stinking Magnificence."

Agonostis' eyes narrowed. "Sir," he snarled. "Call me *sir*, you twittering excrescence, or . . ." But no. He didn't want to rip the imp to shreds. "Or . . ." But he couldn't bake him and feed him to gargoyles either. "Or," he said coldly, ". . . else."

"Sir." The imp's head bobbed up and down like a soul in lava. "Yes, sir, sir."

Imps were up there at the top—with computers—on Agonostis' list of least favorite things.

Agonostis said, "Good. Then starting tomorrow, at zero hour, find a phone and answer it. Don't report back to me until I call you."

"Any phone?"

"Any phone!"

It was too late to find Dayne Kuttner this day—though he knew Lucifer would count the day against his number. He would have to use his first night on Earth just to bring his people in and get them organized. But he could come up with a plan for the corruption of the Almighty's little favorite as he prepared his troops for battle—the next day would be soon enough to start his attack, if he knew in advance how he would run it.

Agonostis decided to get a good look at his surroundings terrain—he felt he ought to be dressed for that; in both a human body and human clothes. He could walk around, get a feel for the type of action in his neighborhood, maybe come up with a few little sidelines the Fiend Downstairs couldn't find out about, figure out ways to skim a nice piece of the action off the top without getting caught. . . .

He smiled. After all the time he'd spent in slow-time doing inventory, he felt like death fried and diced, but Earth air was invigorating stuff . . . and the limitless possibilities in his new situation excited him.

He strolled to the suit rack to outfit himself. He'd counted the suits before, along with the dresses and boxes of shoes, but he hadn't even really looked at any of them. He looked now, and recoiled in horror. There were hundreds of them, in all sizes—and every suit was a wide-lapeled polyester leisure suit, each in colors apparently deemed fashionable in Hell. Lava Orange, Gangrene Green, Boil Red, Bruise Purple, and a number of colors so ugly Agonostis thought he was better off leaving them nameless. All of the jackets were the kind with zippers.

All the socks were white sport socks.

All the shoes were black, thick-soled, and blunt-toed; and they came in two widths—extra-extra wide, and extra-extra narrow.

The ties had been scientifically designed not to match any of the suits, and the shirts . . .

He looked at those shirts and shuddered. Polyester knit Hell-waiian prints. He wondered which damned designer had been put to work on them.

The female clothing, now that he looked at it, was equally dreadful. He was going to have to use a lot of his precious cash to outfit his leccubi in halfway indecent clothing. But more importantly, he was going to have to come up with something sexy for himself.

There was no way in Hell, he decided, that the Lord of Lust would wear polyester. Not to a first meeting, anyway.

He wished he'd been able to find out something about Dayne Kuttner—he wanted to have an idea of what she'd find attractive in a man. He didn't know how old she was or what she looked like—or even if she was married. It would be just his luck that she was pushing the century mark, and faithfully married for the last eighty years.

He manifested himself into the shape of an overweight, red-faced, middle-aged human, put on one of the horrible leisure suits, and grimaced when he discovered the pants were two inches too short, so that his white socks nearly glowed in the dim light of the warehouse.

He shortened his legs by two inches—and the hems of the pants shrank by two more inches.

"Right," he muttered. Clothes from Hell. The only thing to do with them was burn them—and he wasn't even sure they would burn. Such clothing would be fine for devils, and even a step up if worn by demons— but *he* was going to have to go shopping. First thing in the morning.

Chapter 13

Agonostis knew about malls. Malls were Sin Central. People met there for assignations, and lied and cheated and stole and lusted in malls. He didn't know who had come up with the idea for them, but he was sure it was one of Hell's own.

With the pockets of his hellish puce polyester leisure suit stuffed full of cash, he materialized out in the parking lot of one of Charlotte's larger, newer malls at ten A.M. on Saturday morning, just as the doors opened to the public. He'd spent the night working, but that was of no consequence to him. While he needed to eat to maintain his body's health, so far it seemed that he didn't actually need to sleep.

He was alert, he was in good spirits, and he was confident that before the day was out, he and the rest of his crew would hold the state of North Carolina firmly by the testicles.

He waddled into the mall, and immediately earned the stares and giggles of teenaged girls, and the shocked sidelong glances and poorly disguised smirks of their mothers.

No matter, he told himself. The short, fat, balding puce-clad persona was only the creation of a moment, and as a research vehicle, it would do. He bought a newspaper from one of the newsstands, settled himself on a bench, and pretended to read. Thus obscured, he was able to watch the people who passed by him. He observed, and he learned.

Tall, square-jawed men in their late thirties, dressed in expensive suits, drew the glances of well-dressed, upper-class women. Boys in baggy T-shirts and ripped jeans and backwards-turned baseball caps attracted the admiring stares of the silly little girls.

But only one man who passed him turned every female head. The man was young—perhaps twenty-five, certainly no more than twenty-eight. He was a superb physical specimen, tallish, well-muscled but certainly not overly so, with an attractive face. His dark hair was short and neatly styled; he wore his white oxford shirt with the sleeves rolled up and tucked into neat, new-looking blue jeans. He wore a pair of leather deck shoes without socks.

Agonostis thought that sort of appearance would suit him well enough, at least until he'd had a chance to check out Dayne Kuttner. If she turned out to be eighty, he'd come up with another plan. If she didn't turn out to be eighty, he'd gauge her response to him and, if necessary, try again as somebody else.

He found a store that sold men's casual clothing and waddled inside. A cute, pert little sales clerk eyed him doubtfully and said, "May I . . . help you . . . sir?" She paused. "There's a men's large and tall just around the corner."

She smelled delicious. He thought it was a shame he couldn't hurt humans—he imagined she would taste much better than imp. He looked up at her and said, "I'm looking for something for my . . . son. He's a tall boy—about six feet, I suppose. Thin. Lots of muscles."

He watched one of her eyebrows raise, and from the

tiniest of twitches at the corner of her mouth, he realized she was considering that his son most likely wasn't. "Do you have any idea what size he wears?"

"His mother buys things for him most of the time."

"Ah." She sighed. "I don't know how I can help you if you don't know what his sizes are."

"I see." Agonostis walked back to the wall of shelves with those soft blue jeans folded from floor to ceiling. He studied the rows of numbers, growing increasingly more frustrated as he studied them. Finally he snapped, "Just what are these numbers supposed to *mean*?"

She walked back, the expression on her face pure disbelief. "Sir, what size do you . . ." She stared at the hems of his pants, still a good two inches above his shoe tops, and at his jacket with the sleeves too long by the same proportions, and she shook her head, bemused. "Never mind. The number on the left is the waist size. The number on the right is the inseam size— the length from the top of the inside of your leg to the top of your shoe."

"So little numbers on the left and big numbers on the right are better than the other way around."

She was having a hard time keeping a straight face. "Most people choose them by whether they fit or not, not by whether the numbers are better or worse."

"That would explain a lot," he muttered. He found some pants with a smallish waist number and a long inseam, and a white shirt, size Large—that at least was simple enough—and went up to the counter to pay.

"If you keep the tags, you can bring those back," the clerk said. "In case they don't fit."

"They'll fit," he grumbled.

She was grinning as he walked away.

He stopped in a shoe store, and looked up at the clerk there—also a woman, also taller than him. "What is an average shoe size for a man six feet tall?" he asked her.

"Just in general?" she asked.

"Yes . . . just in general."

"Are you doing a survey?"

"No," he snapped. "I'm buying a pair of shoes."

"Why don't we measure your feet—"

"I don't *want* to measure my feet. I want some shoes that will look right on somebody six feet tall."

She sucked on her bottom lip and turned away—he heard her snicker as she led him to the displays.

"Twelve or thirteen is probably about right," she said. "I mean, you know what they say about the sizes of feet and the size of other things. . . ."

That he knew. He found a pair of leather shoes in a size thirteen, average width, had her box them, and strolled to the nearest restroom.

Agonostis knew about restrooms, too—as a matter of fact, he knew all sorts of truly wicked things about restrooms; but the thing he knew that would serve him at the moment was that restrooms were good places to change.

He doubted that many people changed as completely as he intended to, of course.

He found a stall and unwrapped the clothing. He undressed, and stretched himself tall and thin. He had no real idea how tall or how thin—he just guessed. He pulled the pants up and discovered that he'd been extreme in both directions. He filled out a bit, making sure to add sculpted muscle to his legs as he shortened them. He tugged on the shirt and broadened his shoulders and muscled his arms until the cloth was snug there. He made his stomach flat and perfectly muscled. He fumbled with the buttons—*nothing* in Hell had buttons.

He rolled the sleeves up, and resized the muscles of his forearms until he liked the way they looked. He unbuttoned the top two buttons.

Chest hair? He looked down at his slick chest. Yes—he thought so. And hair on the forearms, too. He studied his hands. They were still the fat-fingered hands of Leisure Suit Louie; he lengthened them, and made them strong, and gave them calluses. He studied the fingernails—he was going to miss his own needle-tipped talons, but those simply wouldn't go with the look. He thought blunt, broad, and very clean—kept trimmed short. The hands of a male model.

Face. He needed a good face. He didn't want to look like anybody else; no movie star faces, no jet setters. He needed his own face.

He tried to recall the planes of his face when he'd still been one of Heaven's angels. It was dangerous to think back to that time. More than one of Hell's angels, in a fit of reminiscing, had ended up backsliding enough to win Lucifer's fury and a one-way trip to the Pit. But it had been, he recalled, an exceptionally fine face.

Long, sharp, narrow nose; full lips; even, perfect teeth; strong jaw. He gave himself thick, slightly wavy black hair cut short but full on top, arching black brows, and, for just that extra touch of the unusual, he made his eyes the rich golden-brown color of Russian amber.

He dumped the Hellwear into his shopping bag, and tossed the shopping bag into the trashcan. He studied himself at the mirror in front of the sink, and smiled. He was gorgeous . . . if he did say so himself. He looked like he was in his early twenties, with a vaguely southern European cast to his features.

D'Agonostis, he decided. Adam D'Agonostis. Who could possibly distrust a hot-looking guy named Adam? And the corollaries to temptation, damnation and original sin were so amusing.

He strolled back into the main mall, and smiled as women nearly walked into walls staring at him. This was definitely the look. He wondered what time it was—he needed a watch.

He found a jewelry store that sold Rolexes and bought a solid gold one. That set him back a hefty chunk, but the Rolex was understated, and spoke of both wealth and power. He liked it. The woman who sold it to him was amusing, too. She flirted with him, he flirted back—then he tempted her into the men's room and screwed her in one of the stalls. Afterward, because it amused him, he looked up the girls who sold him the clothes and the shoes, and followed suit with them. They were all willing—more than willing.

He smiled, walking out of the mall.

Dayne Kuttner wouldn't know what hit her.

Chapter 14

Eleven A.M. Zero hour. North Carolina got the first jolt from an unexpected red-hot poker.

CeeCee McAllister, spending her weekend at the beach, was in the tub taking a bubble bath and reading *Cosmopolitan*. The article was great—"How to Tell If He's Good In Bed BEFORE You Hit the Sheets." She was running through the list of men she knew but didn't know quite as well as she might, applying the quiz questions to them.

The phone on the stand beside the tub rang.

She sat up to answer it.

Something hideous and blue with enormous ears pinched her nipple, picked up the phone, and said cheerfully, "Suzy McAllister Sex for Less—do you wanna get laid today?"

Then, while she was still screaming, it handed the phone to her and blinked out of existence.

In the master bedroom of a nice little two-story bungalow in the northern part of the state, Mac Garret and his client, Tanya Bayer Sidonns, soon to be Tanya Bayer again, were screwing their brains out. Mac loved his female divorce clients—so many of them hadn't had attention in years, and if he so much as smiled kindly at them, they were ready to do whatever he wanted.

Tanya wasn't bad. She was a nice enough looking woman, if a bit long in the tooth—but from the back, he thought, pumping away, who noticed teeth?

The phone rang.

"Let it ring," Tanya muttered.

"Uh . . . . huh . . ." he managed by way of answer.

It rang again.

It didn't ring a third time.

Both of them froze as they heard the characteristic click of a phone being lifted from its cradle. Then a rich, beautiful contralto said, "Of course, Mr. Siddons. She has her skirt up around her ears right now and her lawyer is doing unspeakable things to her, but I'm sure she'll be willing to come to the phone in a few minutes. Would you like to wait until he comes, or would you rather call back?"

A *thing* sat on the nightstand—a disgusting blue thing with a malicious grin on its face. It waggled its ears at them and said into the receiver, "Ooop, not a problem now! I think his willy went wooshy. Hang on."

It dropped the phone on the floor and disappeared into thin air.

In a filthy, seedy, city apartment, an answering machine rang the third time.

Earwax picked it up, but said nothing.

"I thought you'd gotten stupid and tried to run. Where's the stuff?" The voice might have belonged to Godzilla. Maybe King Kong. The steroid monster attached to it, Earwax thought, probably didn't weigh less than three, maybe four hundred pounds.

The tenant of the apartment, at that moment, stoned out of his skull and passed out in the bedroom, didn't top a hundred. Earwax said, "I'll have it at my place in fifteen minutes, you freaking pervert. If you want it, you'll have to come in and get it."

"Where the hell are you?"

"You don't know?" Earwax frowned, blinked to the outside of the building, then back in again. "534-D Sunrise Terrace Apartments, on Beecher Street."

"If you don't have it this time, you little shit, I'm going to turn you into sausage."

"By all means, you pimple on the ass of the universe. Your father screwed sheep and your mother went baaaa," Earwax told the thug, and hung up.

He adored his new job.

Chapter 15

Downstairs, someone knocked at her door.

Dayne opened one eye and squinted at the clock across the room.

"Noon?" she muttered. "It's *noon*?"

Paige hadn't been kidding when she said they were going to be up late over at her place. Dayne hadn't gotten home until nearly four A.M.—but she'd had a wonderful time. The man they'd had over for her to meet had been very nice and very funny, and if neither of the two of them were at all interested in each other, everyone had still had a great time.

And the steaks had been delicious.

Porthos stood on the edge of her mattress, glaring at her. He took doors very seriously, and obviously felt she damned well ought to go downstairs and answer this one.

Another polite rap, then whoever was out there tried the doorbell.

Dayne rolled out of bed, pulled on the robe that lay across her reading chair, and peeked out her window.

"Oh, my God," she murmured. The man on her landing deserved to be in the Babedom Hall of Fame. He had great shoulders and a narrow waist. He had long, lean legs. He was young. He was handsome.

He was leaving.

"No-no-no-no-no!" she yelped. She fumbled with the latch on her window, and pulled out the nails to either side that pegged it in place, and pounded with one fist all around the frame until the blasted thing unstuck, and shoved it up, and leaned out, panting slightly.

The racket she'd made trying to get the window open had alerted the gorgeous stranger, and he stood just off the landing, waiting, looking up at her.

"Hi," she said, feeling rumpled and rather silly leaning out her window in her bathrobe. "Can I help you?"

He smiled up at her, and her heart did a skittering little tap dance against her ribs. "I'm so sorry," he said. "I didn't mean to wake you up."

It was that obvious? She winced inside—her hair was probably sticking up in a hundred directions. "I should have been up ages ago," she said, praying that he wouldn't feel so guilty about bothering her that he'd leave. Then she considered . . . it was noon on a Saturday. Maybe he was going door to door selling something.

She shrugged. She hadn't bought anything lately. Maybe she should. She smiled encouragingly. "What did you need?"

His eyes had been fixed on her face, and she realized he was watching her lips move. "Um . . ." he said, and she saw him start just a little. "Oh." He looked into her eyes and—Lord have mercy—he blushed. "My car broke down." He pointed back over his shoulder, and she looked behind him.

A forest-green Porsche convertible with a tan interior sat beneath the willow oak in front of her apartment, its hood up. A thin trail of black smoke curled up from the engine. Black smoke, Dayne knew, tended to be a lot more expensive than white smoke where cars were concerned. "That looks pretty bad," she told him.

He nodded. "I was hoping you wouldn't mind making a call for me. My auto club should be able to send someone right out to get it."

"I'll be happy to," Dayne told him. "Have a seat on the bench—it will take me just a minute, but I'll be right down."

"Sure." He nodded, and smiled again. "Thanks."

Dayne closed the window and beat her head gently against the wall a few times. Usually she got up with the sun. Actually, she frequently beat the sun out of bed by an hour or more.

"Why did I have to be a slob today?" She could have been up, showered, dressed . . .

She rummaged through the clean clothes she'd bothered to wash and fold *and* carry all the way up the stairs—a small subset of the clothing she owned. She found some clean jeans and a V-neck T-shirt that always made her eyes look bluer, and threw them on. At barest minimum, she had to brush her teeth and her hair—she ran to the bathroom and groaned at her first sight of herself. Her hair, shoulder-length, blunt-cut, and black, had that definitely lived-in look.

"Lived in by rodents, maybe," she snarled, bending over and yanking her brush through it at top speed. She brushed her teeth in high gear, scrubbed her face without even letting the water warm up from doing her teeth—so that at least she was much more awake afterward than she had been before—and with one more disgusted look at herself in the mirror, she ran down the stairs.

She snagged the pepper gas off her shelf—paranoia was the better part of virtue, after all—and opened the door.

He stood when he heard it open, and turned and smiled at her. He was even better-looking up close. "This is very nice of you," he told her. He handed her a slip of paper. "This is the number to call. This is my account number. My name is Adam D'Agonostis."

"Dayne Kuttner." Dayne held out her hand, and Adam shook politely. He had a firm grip, but not so hard it was obvious he was trying to prove something. His palm was warm and dry and slightly rough. Sexy. He had the most fascinating eyes she'd ever seen. She'd bet his driver's license said brown, but his eyes were brown the way the sun was yellow. They were, she decided, more of a honey gold that shaded to black at the edge of the iris; they were fringed by thick black lashes. She thought she would find it easy to get lost staring into those eyes. She looked away, down at his car. "No problem. So what happened?"

"I wish I knew. I was driving along this street, I heard a 'pop' and suddenly the dashboard lit up like a pinball machine and black smoke poured out from under the hood." He sighed. "What a way to start my first day in town."

Dayne looked back at him—he was laughing slightly at his trouble. At himself. She doubted she would be either so cheerful or so charming if her car had died on her in the middle of a new city on a Saturday.

She looked down at the paper in her hand. "Let me call these folks and get you some help." She took a deep breath. "I'll have to ask you to wait on the porch. . . ."

He grinned. "Sensible of you. And I don't mind a bit. It's beautiful out today."

She nodded. "Can I get you some tea?"

"I'll be fine," he assured her. "I'm just going to go see if I can get some idea of what blew."

Dayne watched him bound down the steps, and all she could think was, "He's perfect." As she turned to go inside and make his call for him, she became acutely aware, for the first time in years, of precisely how long it had been since she'd last been kissed.

Chapter 16

Agonostis leaned over his trunk and whispered into the air, "Is everything ready?"

Earwax was not present in body, but his voice filtered out of the engine as if he had been. "Oh, hail, Mighty Seducer of Virgins and Deflowerer of the Pure and Innocent. The Devils' Engineering Corps just finished tapping into the main lines, and our telephone guy has us hooked into the eight-hundred system. What number did you give her?

"1-800-462-4355."

"Okay. Got it." Agonostis heard him repeating the number to someone nearby. "Strange number. How did you choose that one?"

"Because it's 1-800-GO2-HELL." Agonostis chuckled. "I thought it was pretty funny."

There was a long, wary silence from Earwax. Then, tentatively, it said, "I thought you guys didn't have senses of humor."

Agonostis stopped chuckling and stared into the motor. The Fallen *didn't* have senses of humor. The Lower Orders—devils, demons, imps and so on—occasionally did, though the humor tended to the dark and the sadistic. The Fallen, though, when an angry God had ripped them from the glorious embrace of Heaven and thrown them into damnation and torture, had lost any semblance of humor from their make-ups.

That Agonostis had come forth with something resembling humor, at least in its outward appearance, and worse, that he had failed to notice he'd done so, unnerved him. After millennia of feeling sure he knew himself perfectly, he looked at that single error as if it were a door opening into a long, twisting, secret passage. He didn't have the nerve to follow it to see where it led.

He said, "It probably wasn't funny anyway."

Earwax, strangely, said nothing at all.

Chapter 17

"Well, I don't like that at all." Heaven's Chief of Data Processing watched his monitor and frowned. "She likes him—and you see what he's already done to those other women today." The angel shook his head nervously. "It simply doesn't seem fair—*he* has supernatural abilities and all the forces of Hell at his command, and she's alone, and doesn't have anything special to fight him with." The angel glanced at God to see if He was taking this as a criticism. "Seems to me you ought to do something to help her out."

God smiled slyly. "She's a big girl . . . figuratively speaking. She can take care of herself."

"Against all of Hell?"

"Well, if there were any sure things, life wouldn't be very interesting for them, would it?"

The angel frowned. "I don't think whether things are interesting for them or not is the big issue here. It would be a shame for her to end up in Hell."

"Yes. It would. But I can't help thinking she's the sort who will stir things up when she arrives in Heaven." God stared thoughtfully up at the vast canopy of stars above His head. "Maybe if I let him tempt her into Hell, she'd reform things for me when she got there . . . what do you think?"

"Good Lord!" The angel was shocked, until he realized

that God's eyes held a twinkle in them, and that beneath the beard, His smile stretched.

The Almighty said, "I will not interfere in the lives or choices of my children. But I will watch with interest."

Chapter 18

Dayne leaned against the kitchen wall and sighed. "I already gave you people his club number. BSC-6665845-I." She sighed loudly. "Adam . . . D'Agonostis. Capital-D-apostrophe-capital-A-G-O-N-O-S-T-I-S . . . . I already told you that, too . . . . Porsche . . . . He drives a green Porsche. North Carolina plates, um . . . PBJ-4239." She rolled her eyes and made a face at the telephone receiver. "No . . . . The *car* is a Porsche. He didn't wreck it into my *porch* . . . . But I don't want to talk to someone else. I've already talked to three people, and all of them said the next person was the one I was supposed to speak to."

Dayne wondered how these people stayed in business. They were awful. Extremely bad Muzak played on the phone line. A new voice came on. This one sounded like Bette Midler. "We can't find him in the computer, honey," she said, and snapped her gum loudly into the receiver.

"The last four people I talked to told me *they* found him in your blasted computer," Dayne said. She was almost done with trying to sound reasonable. "Will you please just send this poor man a tow truck, so he doesn't have to sit on my front porch all day? . . . No! Please don't put me on hol . . ." She held the phone in the air and glared at it, then turned to Porthos and Athos, who sat watching her, twin expressions of interest on their furry faces. "She put me on hold."

Dayne was listening to more of the dreadful Muzak when Paige appeared in her kitchen as if by magic, an expression of awe on her face. "Do you have any idea what you have sitting on your front porch?"

Dayne nodded, but put her finger to her lips. "His car broke dow . . . Yes, I'm still here. Laundry? Oh, my God! *No*, I didn't call to check on my laundry. I was talking to someone from the North Carolina Roadways Automobile Club. Hello? . . . Hello?" She rattled the switchhook a couple of times, then hung up the phone and slowly and dramatically beat her head against the wall.

"They hung up on you?"

"They hung up on me."

"What are you doing?"

"Trying to get his auto club to send a tow truck for him. His car died on him right in front of the house."

"The Porsche?"

"That's the car."

Paige said, "You couldn't ask for better if someone had wrapped him up and sent him to you with a bow around him. So are you still planning on continuing your life as a nun?"

Dayne smiled slowly. "He's given me cause to reconsider. However, dish though Adam D'Agonostis is, I don't think I want to talk to these auto club people again."

"He doesn't belong to Triple A?"

"Nope. His membership is with someplace I never heard of—but that's all right, because when I called, they'd never heard of him either. I've been on the phone for nearly ten minutes . . . you heard the last of it."

"It sounded bizarre. Did they actually connect you to a laundry?"

"If they didn't, they connected me to the part of the auto club that washes clothes." She took a deep breath. "I'm going to give this the old nursing school try one more time. While I do, why don't you invite him to come on back here. I hate to leave him sitting out there—there's no telling how much longer this might take. And with you here—and my pepper gas in my pocket—I think we'll be safe enough."

Dayne dialed, Paige disappeared down the hall, and someone on the other end of the phone picked up. "Hello?"

"I'm trying to reach the North Carolina Roadways Automobile Club."

"Certainly, ma'am. What can I do you for?" The voice on the other end of the phone was deep and rich and resonant—a radio announcer voice.

Dayne winced. "One of your member's cars broke down in front of our house. We're trying to get him some help."

"Name?"

"Adam D'Agonostis."

"Customer number?"

"BSC-6665845-I."

"I show that number licensed to a green late-model Porsche. Is that the car in front of your house?"

Dayne smiled. "That's the one."

"Okay. His account is in good standing. If you'll hold just a moment, I'll put you through to our dispatcher, and she'll determine the problem and send the appropriate person to take care of it."

"Of course."

Dayne gave Paige a relieved grin when she walked back into the room. She covered the receiver with her hand and whispered, "I got hold of someone sane."

Behind her, Adam laughed. "NCRAC had a very high

customer satisfaction rating. I've never had to use them before though."

"You may never want to again," Dayne said, her hand still over the mouthpiece. The Muzak died in mid-wail— a kindness, really, and Dayne was grateful for it.

"This is Charlene," the voice on the other end of the phone suddenly shouted in Dayne's ear. "How may I help you?" The woman sounded almost identical to the Lily Tomlin operator character Dayne had seen on Laugh-In reruns. She imagined the voice saying, 'One ringy-dingy . . . . two ringy-dingy . . .'

"I need to have a tow truck sent over to our house for Mr. Adam D'Agonostis."

"Why? Is he broken?"

Dayne laughed. "His car is."

"I was joking. It was a little joke. Address, please."

Dayne gave her the address.

"My I please have your name and phone number so that we can call you if there are going to be delays?"

Dayne gave them to her.

"Dayne Kuttner . . . with two T's and one N?"

"That's right."

"I'm honored to be speaking with you."

"You are?" Dayne tipped her head and frowned. "Why?"

"One ringy-dingy . . . two ringy-dingy. I was making a joke. It was a little joke. We will send someone right over."

Dayne hung up the phone, still frowning. One ringy-dingy . . . two ringy-dingy? Why had the woman said that? "That was truly bizarre," she told Paige. She turned to Adam D'Agonostis and smiled. "But they're sending someone right over."

He sat at the kitchen table, looking gorgeous in a tired way. "I appreciate you helping me out. I mentioned that I'm from out of town. I'm in charge of the branch of a large corporation that's expanding here. I got lost trying to get off of Independence Boulevard—I have no idea where I am right now . . ." He gave Dayne and Paige a sheepish smile.

Dayne grinned. "Don't let Independence bother you. Native Charlotteans know for a fact that there's at least one hyperspatial anomaly intersecting that road. Nobody gets the right turn-off on the first try."

"You knew about that?" Adam frowned.

Dayne laughed—he played along very well. "Anyway, what happened next?"

"My car died," he said. "The day wasn't shaping up to be one of the better ones I've ever had." He smiled, this time just at Dayne. "Though things do seem to be looking up."

Dayne felt her cheeks get hot. Into the awkward silence that followed, she asked, "What sort of corporation do you work for?"

"We deal with computers primarily, though we have interests in a number of other things. We're big, well-diversified . . ." He smiled at nothing in particular and took a sip of his tea. "And expanding."

Paige leaned back on the counter. "My husband works in computers. He's a wizard . . . travels all over the world making other people's systems work."

Dayne noticed the flash of interest in Adam's eyes and in the way he leaned forward in his seat. He looked at Paige as if he had just spotted gold. "A wizard? If you don't mind my asking, how much does he make? What sort of benefits does he get, and what sort would he like? We're way short of computer gurus right now, and hiring. We need top-quality people, and if he has the qualifications we're looking for, I'm in a position to offer him just about anything he wants."

Paige smiled slowly. "I don't know that he wants anything. He likes his job."

Adam shook his head and sighed. "Yeah. They always do."

Dayne noticed that he had fabulous hands, and his forearms were muscular and lightly furred with soft black hair. She found having him in her house delightful. "I hate computers," she said, sitting down in the seat across the table from him.

"Yeah. Me too." He rested his chin on one hand, and she got a good look at his watch. *Rolex? Looked like one. A Rolex, a Porsche, and blue jeans.* He was not the sort of fellow she found on her doorstep most days. He grinned at her.

"You hate computers . . . and you work in a computer firm?"

"I'm the manager. I don't actually have to work with the little bastards . . . excuse me . . . um, machines."

Dayne laughed.

"So . . . Dayne . . ."

She waited.

He smiled. "Dayne Kuttner . . . would it be terribly forward of me if I asked you out?" He glanced at her left hand quickly. "Oh, I'm sorry. You're wearing a ring." He took a deep breath. "I thought . . ." He shook his head and looked out the kitchen window into the tiny backyards of the apartments.

She read disappointment in his face, his eyes, the set of his shoulders.

"I was widowed four years ago," she told him. "As for asking me out, well—" She had, in the past four years, become very good at saying no. Saying yes turned out to be surprisingly tough. "Maybe. I think I'd like that."

Someone out in front of the house laid on an air horn—the blast rattled the windows.

All three people in the kitchen jumped.

"The tow truck—" Dayne said.

"Why did they have to get here so fast?" Adam muttered. Paige hung back and said nothing.

It was indeed the tow truck, driven by someone who was apparently in a great hurry. Whoever it was had just hooked the tow hook under the Porsche's front bumper.

"NOT LIKE THAT!" Adam howled, and took off down the steps and across the apartment lawn as if he'd sprouted wings. Dayne, standing behind her screen door, watched him charge after the idiot with the tow truck and read him the riot act.

"He's going to ask you out," the voice behind her said.

"Paige, I'll believe it when it happens."

"Are you going to be a sane person and accept?"

Dayne turned to look at her friend. "This is the first time in years I've even been interested. If he actually calls me up and asks, I almost certainly will go out with him." She looked at the scene in front of her house, where Adam was showing the man with the tow truck how to tow a Porsche.

"I'm afraid he was just being polite when he said he'd like to call me, though."

Paige shrugged. The tow truck drove off with Adam in it and his dead car following behind. "So let's not think about it. Some of Mike's clients took him to the UNC-Duke game. I didn't want to go, but I thought I'd come over here and you and I could visit . . . and maybe watch a little of it together."

Suddenly Dayne realized that she was tired. "That sounds great." She flopped onto the couch and grabbed the remote, and flipped the TV on. Paige dropped onto the seat beside her.

News. Saturday afternoon news?

Dayne flipped the channel.

News.

An *I Love Lucy* rerun.

PowerLizards, or some such cartoon dreck.

News.

News.

News.

"What the hell—" Paige muttered.

"I don't know." Dayne kept flipping channels. It was two in the afternoon, and CNN should have been the only place with news. "The Charlotte games are usually on Channel 13, but . . ." She saw something football-like flash onto the screen, then off again. She backed up a channel. "Never mind. Here it is."

The Duke Blue Devils and the UNC Tarheels were on the field, and the Tarheel quarterback threw a beautiful long bomb down the field. His wide receiver ran a terrific pattern, was in the right spot to pick up the pass, was as clear as a Carolina afternoon . . .

And some huge guy in an obscene bright-red devil suit, with a pitchfork, no less, appeared literally out of nowhere and speared the football out of mid-air. With the deflated pigskin skewered on his pitchfork, he ran straight through the oncoming Tarheels, blasted his way through the Blue Devils, charged alone up the field into the Blue Devil end zone, and did a victory dance that involved gestures someone managed to cover with strategically placed boxes.

"And that was the scene an hour ago right here in Charlotte. Following riots and some injuries, the game was cancelled—the cancellation declared an act of God. Somehow those words seem to mean more than they ever did."

"Riots. Oh, my God," Paige yelped. "I've got to call home." She ran for the telephone.

Carlston Perry, the anchorman for *Channel Six at Six*, stood panting in front of the camera—his usually perfect hair was mussed and his shirtsleeves were rolled up. His tie was crooked. "All across the state, we have similar reports. We take you live to Treya Billingsley at the Ashboro Fan Faire in Ashboro, North Carolina, where two deaths have been confirmed."

Treya Billingsley stood in front of a brick building where an ambulance sat, lights flashing. Her face held that fake-grim expression television reporters always seemed to wear when they were reporting on something exciting, but thought it would look crude if anyone could tell they were enjoying themselves. EMTs pushed crowds of people out of the way and shoved out sheet-covered stretchers, but Treya and the cameras kept going. "Thank you, Carlston. The final event of the Ashboro Fan Faire, the White Plectrum Filk concert, ended in tragedy today when Bill Mullis and Keith Brinegar, in the middle of their rendition of Leon Redbone's classic, 'I Wanna Be Seduced,' were set upon by a bevy of what seemed to be nude women who attempted to seduce them right on stage. What would have been merely a shocking incident became a disaster as hundreds of male fans, tempted beyond restraint, ran forward and attempted to join in. Klingon security officers and men and women in Star Fleet uniforms acted quickly to restore order, but by the time they cleared away the last of the young men, it was too late to save either Mullis or Brinegar."

"I think it's the way they would have wanted to go," one tearful White Plectrum fan told her in a taped segment. "Crushed beneath a pile of naked women— it just seems right somehow."

Treya tactfully refrained from commenting that the crush came not from the naked women, but from the fans who'd piled on top of them.

The camera cut back to Treya live. "The women, caught beneath the pile, turned out to be neither injured . . . nor women. In this interview, taped earlier,

I talk with one, who claims she is a succubus straight from Hell."

Dayne could hear Paige in the other room, talking on the phone. ". . . just as long as you're okay."

Good. So Mike hadn't been hurt. Dayne stared off into space. What were the odds? Could there be a connection between her prayer and the arrival of devils and demons to North Carolina. It didn't seem likely— after all, she couldn't really see where it would be necessary to turn Hell's creatures loose in order to permit them to repent.

But maybe it was. She had no way of knowing, and decided she'd do best to adopt a wait-and-see attitude. After all, sooner or later someone would figure out what was going on.

She'd missed the interview with the succubus. Instead, a Fayetteville reporter was leading off her story with the line, "Halloween came early this year," while the scene switched to packs of candy-colored little imps that ran from door to door through a pretty neighborhood, ringing doorbells and soaping windows and dumping sugar into gas tanks.

There was more. There was much, much more.

Chapter 19

Agonostis strolled into his "office." Earwax met him at the door. "Did I do okay, sir?"

"For now." Agonostis looked around what had, the night before, been an abandoned warehouse. Rows of hastily erected cubicles (the Hell-bound were big on cubicles) filled the center of the floor. Computer cables snaked across the cracked concrete, running to special terminator boxes that linked them straight to Hell's mainframes.

The Real Estate Devil scurried up to him and said, "We own the building now—in fact, we own the entire block. We've thrown out the winos and the drug dealers and started fixing up the building next door. It will take some work, but I think we can make it respectable enough to use as a front."

Agonostis nodded. "Good. Continue." The Real Estate Devil hurried off.

"They fixed you up a temporary office in the back," Earwax said. "I think you'll approve. It has a great view of the hookers working the neighborhood."

"There are hookers—working *this* neighborhood!" Jezerael, who had taken Lust and Fornication away from him with her damned plotting, was making points with every one of those hookers. "Chase them down to the Salvation Army," he snapped. "Or call the police and have them arrested."

Jezerael was not going to get any freebies from him.

Earwax was still standing at his knee, waiting for . . . something. Who knew what went through the microscopic minds of imps?

"What are you waiting for?"

Earwax started. "Er . . . orders?"

He needed to have someone keep an eye on Dayne. "Fine. Here are some orders. Put a tap on Dayne Kuttner's phone. Then I want you to personally watch her house. Find out for me everything she does, every place she goes, every person she talks to."

"Can I answer her phone?"

"*No*, you can't answer her phone! She isn't supposed to know you're there."

He was forgetting something else . . . something important. . . .

The pets. "Don't bother her cats, either. No one had better touch those cats until I give the okay."

Earwax nodded, his expression mournful. "No cats. No phones. No fun." He trudged away, shoulders sagging.

Agonostis smiled and walked through his new domain. All his damned were busy, Hell Phase II was opening for business, and Dayne Kuttner was putty in his hands. The first phase of her temptation had gone remarkably well. He'd assumed he would have to make at least two trips by her home to find a form that would prove irresistible to the woman; to have hit his stride in one was, he thought, simply proof of his suitability for his role as Lord of Lust.

Jezerael would be out of a job before she knew what had hit her.

And spunky little wide-eyed Dayne would be writhing in Hell.

Agonostis' smile grew bigger.

Chapter 20

Dayne sat transfixed by the news. It preempted every local station's regular programming, and clips from the local news began showing up on the national news, as well—generally as the lead story.

As the reports of chaos poured in, a few themes became clear. The Hellraised (a phrase coined early by one clever reporter, and instantly dragged into general use) were raising Hell and upsetting things as much as they could—but they weren't killing people. The two men who died at the Ashboro Fan Faire were the only reported deaths in what news stations across the state were claiming were thousands of reported incidents— and their deaths were the result not of the actions of the Hellraised, but of their human fans.

"So where do you think they came from?" Paige asked.

"Hell."

"Don't be obtuse. How do you think they *got* here?"

"Oh." Dayne sat on the edge of the couch and stared at the TV screen—at the camera shots of devils and demons and imps and gargoyles; of incubi and succubi and gremlins. Bemused, she said, "I think God has given them a second chance."

Paige turned sideways on the couch and gave Dayne a half smile. "Come again?"

"I'd rather not say anything until I know for sure. . . ."

She wrinkled her nose and made a face at Paige. "I'll be very interested to know why they're here."

"Me too." Paige fished the last of the buttery kernels of popcorn from the bottom of the bowl and shook her head. "Mike said everyone thought the devils on the football field were a Duke prank at first. They ran out from the locker rooms and started doing cheers with the Tarheel cheerleaders. Then they started goosing the cheerleaders with their pitchforks. Security tried to run them off, they turned and charged the security officers, and Mike said all of a sudden they grew like three or four feet taller and got these huge claws and bat wings. Mike said it was the scariest thing he ever saw. The people in the stands had been laughing, but then they stopped, and a lot of them tried to run for the exits."

"What did Mike do?"

"He and his clients stayed put, and they were fine. A few people were hurt, nobody seriously."

"I'm surprised he didn't want you to come home."

Paige shook her head. "He and his clients decided to discuss business at the house. Less excitement. I'm sure he'd love to have me there, but I hate discussions of LANs and RISCs and RAM and such." She wrinkled her nose. "About as much as he hates to hear me talk about FHA and HUD and points and features."

"I'll bet. You two make a strange couple."

Paige nodded. "We have fun. The things we have in common make up for the fact that we can't really talk about work."

"Things in common? Like—"

"We're both horny little devils. . . ." Paige pulled her knees up to her chest and wrapped her arms around her legs. The smile vanished from her face. "That isn't actually funny anymore," she said softly. "When nobody thought it was real, Hell was kind of a funny place. People told devil jokes and—said 'damn it' and never really considered what 'damn it' meant. But now . . ." She sighed. "Everything has changed. The fundamentalists and the Jesus-shouters were right." She frowned. "All the things we thought we knew, maybe we didn't know after all." She got up and said, "I need something to drink. I'll be right back."

She walked down the hall to the kitchen. Dayne watched her, and said quietly into the empty room, "I never thought Hell was a funny place. Not ever."

Channel 13 switched from commentary and speculation to Toni Spellman doing an interview live in front of the City Hall in Charlotte.

"We have with us Mr. Roiling Pusbucket," the reporter said, and Dayne turned her attention to the news. Roiling Pusbucket?

"Paige!" she yelled. "Get in here! They're going to interview a devil!"

Paige ran in, holding a Diet Coke in one hand and a bag of chips in the other. She dropped onto the couch again, and popped the top on the Coke.

"Mr. Pusbucket claims he is high on Hell's chain of command, and he has kindly granted us an interview."

A scaly-faced demon, in a leisure suit so loud Dayne tried to readjust the color of her television set just to tone it down, smiled at the reporter. "Thank you, Toni. Greetings from Hell."

Toni's smile was forced. "Thank you, Mr. Pusbucket."

"You can call me Roiling."

"Roiling, then. Millions of people are watching you, right now, and wondering what you are doing here. How did you get here? Do you have a mission? How long are you going to be here?"

Roiling Pusbucket chuckled and rested a hand on Toni's shoulder—Dayne watched the reporter shrink back, and the demon's hand dropped to his side.

"Well, Toni . . . I'm pleased to say that we are here in North Carolina by the grace of the Almighty. We don't have a time limit set on our parole—as far as I know, we've been turned loose for good. God decided to give us all a second chance; you know, a chance to repent—"

"Why would God *do* that?" Toni interrupted.

The demon grinned. "I'll get to that in a moment."

Toni nodded. "So what is your mission?"

The demon grinned. "I reckon God is hoping we'll all convert. But the Boss let us know our mission is the usual. Drum up business for the Corporation, bring in the revenues—"

"By the Corporation, I assume you mean Hell. And revenue would be souls," Toni interrupted. "Souls damned to Hell."

"Sure. That's what the Corporation does. Well, cash too. Every business needs a good cash flow. But we need cash, and we need product. We've been in the business a long time, missy—and it's good work. I've made it all the way from damnedsoul up to demon third class—should make devil junior grade in six months, if I can turn a decent profit."

"You get promoted. For dragging people into Hell." This concept looked like it bothered the reporter a lot.

"Honey, we don't drag 'em. Most of 'em come running." The demon scratched absently at his crotch. "Hell is very democratic—promotions based on merits, demotions based on demerits. . . ." He grinned broadly. "If you like dictatorships, go to Heaven. No room for advancement there—whatever you are when you get there, that's what you're going to be for all eternity. But if you like challenges, if you crave adventure, if you want to be all you can be, then Hell's the place for you."

"Is it just coincidence that Hell sounds an awful lot like the Army?"

" 'Course not. We recruit heavily from the military. You'd be surprised the number of ex-privates who have the pleasure of running their old drill sergeants through the hoops." The demon shrugged. "But you're missing the point. Hell is more than fire and brimstone. We research markets, we create new products, we compete in the open marketplace with the Old Communist. We hustle. We grow."

"Were you referring to God as the Old Communist?"

"Mr. 'Each-According-To-His-Needs.' That's the one. If you desire more out of life than just what somebody else thinks is your fair share, you don't want to go to Heaven. Request Hell when it's time to punch your ticket."

"Mr. Pusbucket—"

"Roiling, honey. Just call me Roiling."

"I think I prefer Mr. Pusbucket. It is obvious that whatever God may have hoped for when he released you, you have no intention of acceding to his wishes. So why did he turn you loose? Why would God set— how many of you are there?"

"Fifty-eight thousand eight hundred fifty-one."

The reporter didn't answer so much as she sort of gurgled in the back of her throat.

"That's a lot," Paige said.

Dayne nibbled on the inside of her lip. "That's a lot."

The reporter got her voice back. "Why would God set fifty-eight thousand plus Hellraised loose in North Carolina?"

"According to the rules and regs we received, because that was one one-hundredth of the state's population at the time he decided to do it."

"That isn't what I mean. Why did he decide to do it?"

The demon grinned and looked at the camera. Dayne's stomach tightened.

"One of your fellow North Carolinians asked him to. All of Hell is having a big celebration today in honor of Dayne Teresa Kuttner of Charlotte, North Carolina." The devil waved at the camera, and smiled broadly, so that his yellowed, dagger-like teeth gleamed. "Hi, Dayne," he said. "You're our kind of person!"

Dayne closed her eyes and shoved her head back against the couch.

"Oh . . . my . . . God . . ." Paige said. She turned and stared at Dayne. "What did you *do*?"

"Oh boy," Dayne whispered. "Oh boy oh boy oh boy."

"What are you *going* to do?"

"He listened," Dayne said. "I mean, I believed He listened, but He really, truly, honestly listened . . . and He did it." She started smiling. She opened her eyes. "Paige—God did it."

"I'll say. He threw you into the soup up to your neck."

"No-no-no. You don't understand. I mean God gave them all second chances. *All* of them. Now nobody has to suffer. Not Lucifer. Not his devils and demons." She closed her eyes as she felt the tears filling them. "Not Torry. No one ever has to be trapped in Hell anymore."

Paige said, "Dayne, that's great. The denizens of Hell aren't trapped in Hell. That's good news, I'm sure." Her voice was dry and gravelly. "The bad news, though, is that now Hell's damned are in North Carolina."

She took a deep breath and added, "And the really bad news is that it's all your fault. If you were going to pick one thing not to do in the Bible Belt—I'm just guessing here, you understand, but my guess is—that would be the thing."

Chapter 21

Paige went home at last, expressing some concern about stepping out the door. Dayne locked the door and the deadbolt and the night lock and started closing up for the night. She couldn't see any sense in staying up later. Nothing new was happening on the devil front—the reporters had stopped doing many live spots, and now the commentators were on the air, telling the world what it all meant. She figured she had a better idea than they did of what it meant, so it seemed like a good time to get some sleep.

Besides, she had Sunday off. Two days in a row . . . and for once, she was going to get both of them. She intended to let the answering machine take all her calls. She was going to get some more sleep, and she knew if anyone in the unit called in, the nursing supervisor would call and ask her to come in to work.

She'd just turned off the kitchen lights and was getting ready to run upstairs when her doorbell rang.

"Paige?" she wondered. Paige frequently forgot things . . . like her purse or her house keys or something else equally essential. Dayne turned on the porch light, then peeked through the peephole in the door.

It wasn't Paige. It was a reporter, standing with his back to her on her landing, while a cameraman fiddled with lights and his range.

It was a bit late for reporters, she thought, but she could understand the enthusiasm. *Maybe if I talk to this one, the rest will let me sleep in a little tomorrow.*

She opened the door and smiled. "Hi. Can I help you?"

The reporter turned, looked over her head, then looked down. A cold smile crossed his face. "Miss Kuttner?" he asked.

"That's right."

He stepped forward, crowding into Dayne's comfort zone. She backed up, and he followed, so that she stood well into her apartment, while he stood just inside the threshold, holding the door wide open.

"Charlie, on me in three . . . two . . . one . . ."

"This is Marty Fisk, live at the home of Dayne Kuttner, the woman who set Hell loose in North Carolina. Miss Kuttner . . ."

"It's Mrs.," she said. "My name is *Mrs*. Dayne Kuttner."

"Oh." He looked around, his expression slightly nervous, but when Mr. Kuttner didn't appear, he continued. "*Mrs*. Kuttner. Why did you do this terrible thing?"

She frowned. "Mr. Fisk, is it?" He nodded. "This was no terrible thing. It was—it is—a wonderful thing. I prayed for God to give every soul in Hell a second chance," Dayne told him earnestly. "God listened."

"Miss Kuttner, learned scholars believe that with your prayer—if in fact it was a prayer, though we have no proof of that—you have set into motion the evil events of the Final Days. In fact, well-placed and well-informed ministers equate your role with that of the Harlot of Babylon, and suggest that you might in fact be her."

Dayne felt a cold fire begin to burn in her belly. "They do, do they? Remember what Jesus said. Judge not, that you are not judged, Mr. Fisk," she said.

The cameraman grinned and zoomed in closer on her face.

Fisk took another step into her house, and said, "Even the devil can quote scripture. How long have you *been* in communication with the devil?" he demanded.

"Mr. Fisk," Dayne said softly, "I did not invite you in my house, and you are both trespassing and unwelcome. Get out, right now."

"Then you admit to being in league with the devil?"

"Mr. Fisk, I prayed for God to have mercy on every soul, and I hope he has mercy on yours, but if you don't get out of my house right this minute, I'm going to send you to Heaven to talk to him tonight."

The cameraman laughed out loud—one short, sharp bark that died away to silence as Fisk turned and faced the camera. "Satan worshippers and death threats, lies and deceit. We're here live in an interview with the notorious Whore of Babylon . . ." He rested a hand on the little earphone in his ear, listening to a question from his base.

Dayne's right hand brushed against a lump in her jeans pocket. She slipped her hand in, and wrapped it around a cold metal canister. She grinned. Pepper gas. She flipped the safety off, and said, "Mr. Fisk?"

"I'll ask her now," he said in response to the question she couldn't hear. He turned, another question on his lips—and Dayne sprayed him in the face.

He gasped and screamed, and she stomped on the arch of his foot, then rammed one knee up between his legs, and when he buckled forward, slammed her elbow into his nose. Then, coughing and with her own eyes watering, she pointed at the cameraman and gasped, "Get him out of here or you're next."

The cameraman grabbed the reporter and dragged him off, and Dayne stepped back into her hallway, locked the door and bolted it, and ran to the kitchen and stuck her head under the tap and ran water in her eyes.

The insides of her eyelids felt like they were going to melt off, her face was on fire inside and out, and she'd breathed the stuff and couldn't stop coughing. The big problem with pepper gas was that it was almost as tough on the person who used it as on the one it was used on.

"Sorry son of a gun," she muttered. "I guess I know how to deal with reporters now."

She stomped up the stairs. "Whore of Babylon."

She kicked the doorframe—it made a satisfying noise. "Who does he think he is?—Whore of Babylon."

She strangled the toothpaste tube and brushed her teeth as if she were murdering them.

"I'll give *him* the Whore of Babylon."

Chapter 22

Wild laughter interrupted Agonostis' work—he'd been refining and adding to his battle plans. He walked out to the main office to discover that the imps had found a television set and VCR, and had gotten them to work.

"Did it tape? Did it tape?" one shrieked.

Its twin howled, "Rewind! Rewind!"

"It's rewound! Play it! Play it!"

He was going to tell them to turn the TV off when the imps' tape started to run, and he realized the reporter onscreen was interviewing Dayne. She had a great television Q, he noticed—even though she was obviously tired, and obviously angry, she still looked terrific on the idiot box. He leaned against the wall with his hands tucked into the front pockets of his jeans and watched—he would learn something useful about her from the interview.

Moments later, she went from being angry but polite to being furious and dangerous. He saw her reach into her pocket and pull out something, though he couldn't make out what she had. But when the reporter turned and she sprayed in the face with whatever it was, then gave him a couple of well-placed kicks and a punch, Agonostis felt an itch growing between his shoulderblades. She aimed the same weapon at the cameraman, and the last of the picture was of the ground in front of her home bouncing and jostling, and a blurry picture of two sets of stumbling, running feet.

The imps howled and rewound the tape again, and Agonostis walked thoughtfully back into his office.

She'd had that little lump in her pocket when he'd been there.

It had been a weapon.

She wasn't such a trusting soul after all. And he wondered if, in his human form, Dayne could have hurt him badly had he tried something she didn't like. He was from Hell—he was used to pain. Except he hadn't hurt at all since he'd arrived, and not hurting quickly became a pleasant habit. He thought he would be careful to mind his manners in Dayne's presence.

The reporter had been an idiot to present his questions the way he had, but he'd had a nice angle. The Whore of Babylon bit would certainly work well against Dayne, if it were used by someone who knew what the hell he was doing. Agonostis gave some thought to rumors and innuendo he could spread via his coalescing network; he ought to be able to see that she was completely humiliated and discredited within a couple of days. That would break her spirit. From that point on, it would be simple to effect her downfall.

Meanwhile, he had a war to run.

Agonostis picked up his copy of *The Sensitive Male* and flipped through the last several pages. He snorted, disgusted. "Yeah, sure. I could have written this shit. I know dodges this guy never even thought of."

"We're ready, Lord Agonostis."

He put down the book and rested his feet on his desk. "Let's have a look."

The leccubi were ready to get to work. They'd outfitted themselves in bodies as well as clothes—the bodies were spectacular, the clothing good—if expensive—Earth-made stuff.

Moret paraded in first. It was in succubus form, and had designed itself as a pneumatic platinum blonde with black lashes and silvery blue eyes. It wore a see-through blouse, fishnet hose, and a micro-micro miniskirt.

Agonostis nodded. "With that look, Moret, you want more tits. And more of a wiggle. And remember, cash only tonight. We aren't set up for credit cards yet."

Moret nodded and obligingly added about two cup sizes to its breasts.

"Better," Agonostis said, "You want to be sure the buttons are almost ready to pop. Next."

Federet had made itself into a boy, not more than twelve or thirteen. It primped at Agonostis seductively and the fallen angel smiled coldly. "Very good. Very, very good. No doubt at all that you're under age. Take advantage of that."

They paraded past him as males and females, as males dressed as females, as children—wearing leather, lace, neoprene rubber, elegant business suits and evening wear. They were aiming for every segment of the flesh-buying market, and Agonostis thought they were going to be quite a hit.

He didn't have to worry about Jezerael getting credit for the sinners his leccubi dragged in; Hell would credit him with every sin won by the onsite team, no matter the method. And in fact, Agonostis thought of a very clever dodge that might permit him to trash Jezerael's numbers and leave her dangling by her talons from the lip of the Pit.

His "whores" would be—as demanded by Heaven's regulations—disease-free. They could not cause physical harm; while he would have preferred the freedom to destroy humans in any manner he saw fit, he could see where in this one instance, that odd little barrier to what he would have preferred might work in his favor.

If he could advertise Heaven-warrantied disease-free whores, he could grab an enormous share of the market.

He stood and paced. It would take clever advertising, and a way to tell his whores from the human variety. . . .

Marketing was definitely the key. The marketing of damnable vice as good, clean, safe fun—that was the ticket. Using all the modern means of advertising at his disposal . . . coming up with an attractive package . . . emphasizing the entertainment value, the novelty value . . . finding a locale where he could control ingress and egress, and make sure no diseased human hookers could contaminate his product. . . .

What he needed, he thought, was sort of an amusement park of a whorehouse.

He stopped stock-still as that thought took hold of him. Why not? Why not! What a marketing concept!

He sat down and began listing the things that could tempt people in, basing the concept on the amusement park idea.

The whores, naturally . . . but the whores were small-time. Screwing wasn't much of a vice unless there was evil in the heart, too. So he needed to inject an element of evil into that aspect of the temptation—something that would subvert his marks. He'd come back to that. But the idea was bigger than whores. The amusement park concept was greatly expandable. He would have to start with rides, of course. He could do something terrific with multiple dimensions, and special effects. There was no real way that he could think of to make the rides into part of the temptation—but they could certainly be part of the draw. Good, clean fun. In North Carolina, water parks went well—summers were hot. Water parks meant girls in bikinis, lots of lust. What was his angle for that? He closed his eyes and took a deep breath. Girls . . . endless vistas of screwable girls. He smiled slowly. A water park with real mermaids.

And mermen. Teasing, taunting, endlessly horny mermaids, always just out of reach. His leccubi could fill those roles.

What else? There were humans who wouldn't ever bother with a water park. How about the scariest haunted house this side of Hell? Monster rides. Riding monsters. But funny . . . play down the horror of Hell. Make it . . . cute.

Instead of a petting zoo—a prehistoric petting zoo. The success of Jurassic Park and its ilk were not lost on him. But with guaranteed safety . . . Oh, yes. That would draw them in. If he were very careful to keep his epochs separate, and to use only the real beasts, he could get the soul of every paleontologist breathing. And when was the last time a paleontologist went to Hell? Not even he could remember.

For the upscale crowd, the best of Broadway and opera, reviving long-dead stars to reprise their most famous roles . . .

Ballerinas (or rather, their perfect simulacrums) brought back from the dead to dance the ballets the viewers most wanted to see, and to meet backstage afterwards with their adoring fans . . .

The return of the best of the jazz musicians, of the rock-and-roll superstars, of the comedians now lost and gone to dust . . .

A historical district, with living historical figures . . .

For the arcade and gaming crowd, a castle full of live-action, alternate-reality gaming—the real thing, with special effects provided by Hell . . .

A body shop, to give people the bodies they'd always wanted . . .

A sports world, that let armchair heroes become the real thing for just a little while . . .

A library of lost books, featuring every book that had been written since the dawn of time. . . .

The ultimate mall, for power-shoppers . . .

A midway . . .

A carnival . . .

A lover's point . . .

Devil's Point. The Amusement Park from Hell. He caught his breath. It was incredible. Who could resist it?

And then he thought of the perfect final draw. The cover price would be a bit less than for any other theme park, and he would do extensive advertising that the cover price was the *only* price. No selling of souls for anything in Devil's Point. The mark would find almost exactly what he wanted in Devil's Point, whatever it was, and he would get it for the cover price, plus the item cost. The things the mark would find would never be quite perfect, but they would be very, very good. Good enough for a while—good enough until the mark wanted more than good enough, and until he wanted it badly enough.

When the mark knew *exactly* what he wanted, and when he wanted it enough that he was willing to do anything to get it . . . he would find a door. The door into Desire Point—the secret part of the amusement park. And behind that door, he would find his heart's desire.

For a slightly higher price.

Chapter 23

SUNDAY, OCTOBER 10TH

Dayne bounded out of bed early on Sunday morning, did a quick workout on the stair-stepper and with her weights, and ignored the ringing of the telephone downstairs—the answering machine could get the phone, because after finishing a seventy-hour work week, she had no intention of going in to help out at the hospital on her day off.

The phone rang at fifteen minute intervals, with some calls closer than that. They must have had a stack of Sunday morning call-ins. She shrugged and climbed into the shower. Life's tough, she thought. She'd worked short-staffed all week and covered everybody else's hours, but if she answered the phone, the supervisor was going to try to make her feel guilty for not coming in to help out on her day off, too.

"Today," she muttered, "the hospital's problems are not my problem."

The phone was still ringing when she got out. "Two options," she thought. "I can unplug it, or I can go someplace."

On such a beautiful October morning, with the sun shining through her kitchen window and the light slanting long, in that peculiar way that signaled autumn, unplugging the phone seemed to her a fool's choice. So she packed a lunch, grabbed her keys and her purse, and headed out her front door . . .

. . . Into the only silent circus she'd ever seen.

She noticed the picketers first; two lines of them worked opposite ends of the sidewalk. The batch on the right were dressed in business suits or neat dresses, and they carried signs that read, "SEND THEM BACK, WE PRAY!" and "NO DEVILS IN MY BACKYARD!" and "THINK OF OUR CHILDREN: NO DEVILS HERE!" and "BAPTISTS AGAINST SATAN!"

The other line consisted of people wearing black. Their signs read "MAKE ROOM FOR DEVILS," and "OUR FATHER WHO ART IN HELL, WELCOME TO NORTH CAROLINA," and "HELL HERE NOW!"

Two men at a hastily set-up card table seemed to have been doing a brisk business in T-shirts—on one, Dayne recognized a fairly good caricature of herself holding a miniature devil by the scruff of the neck with one hand and slapping her forehead with the other. The slogan blazoned across the front read "I Should Have Had a V8." Another had her standing arm in arm with a devil holding a trick-or-treat bag. That one read "Hell for the Holidays."

Uniformed police officers stood beside their cars, some watching the goings-on, and some directing traffic. And the traffic! Nobody honked horns, nobody leaned out of windows and shouted. It was the most polite, orderly mob Dayne had ever seen. She frowned—she couldn't understand the silence. Then her eyes widened as she realized the quietest group of all waited, video cameras trained on her, reporters watching with microphones in hand—studying her warily from just beyond her landing. Everything had stopped when she stepped out of her door, and all eyes were trained on her, and in all of them she saw something she would never have expected.

She saw fear.

They were afraid of her. She walked toward them, and the nearest reporters took a single step back. The walk in front of her cleared, the massed humanity separating neatly and silently as if it were water and she were Moses parting the Dead Sea. The picketers had stopped walking, and stood watching her. The cars in front of the house had come to a halt, and people were leaning out of their windows taking pictures. The police were watching the people in the cars, and she realized with a sick lurch in her gut that they were trying to make sure the only things pointed at her were cameras.

She took another step forward, uncertainly. She couldn't get her car out of its parking place—not in this mob. She looked at the reporters, and one man nervously crossed his legs, and one woman cleared her throat.

"Would you be willing to give a statement to the press?" the woman asked.

Would she? What could she possibly have to say to reporters?

But she nodded, and walked back, and sat on the top step of her landing. She tucked her purse behind her feet and dropped her lunch beside her, and made sure her keys were in her left jacket pocket, and slid her hand over the reassuring weight of the pepper gas canister in her right pocket. "What do you want to know?"

It was the oddest press conference she'd ever seen. The reporters, who had talked fearlessly with the minions of Hell, were circumspect with her. They were polite, and careful, and quiet—and they stayed a good ten feet back from her, though they maneuvered their microphones close. And suddenly she realized that, while the people in the street might be afraid of Dayne Kuttner, the reporters were even more afraid of Dayne

Kuttner's pepper gas, and her knees, and her elbows. That fear was evident in the protective stances the male reporters took.

Dayne grinned. She'd like to know why people did the things they did. As long as she could understand, she could cope. They asked her a few simple questions, taking turns instead of trying to shout each other down. She began to believe all people who were to be interviewed needed to gas the first reporter who approached them and kick him in the nuts. It did wonders for the manners of the rest.

At last they got to the meatier questions. "Would you tell us why you asked God to free Satan's hordes?" one reporter asked.

"I didn't," Dayne said. "I only asked God to give every soul in Hell a second chance. I am no more sure than you are about why he chose to answer my prayer in this fashion. I do have a theory, though."

"What is it?"

"I think perhaps God wants our help." She leaned forward and spread her hands in front of her. "Think of it. The Fallen have been in Hell for eons—we have no way of knowing how long. But they are God's creatures as surely as we are, and certainly he must want them to repent and return to his grace. A father who loves his children could take no pleasure from seeing them in pain. Perhaps he wishes us to show them the things they have been so long without in Hell, to remind them of what they have forsaken."

"What have the Hellraised forsaken, do you think?"

"Friendship," Dayne said softly. "Kindness. Hope. Compassion. Honor." She looked out over the faces that stared into hers. "Love."

"You think God wants us to *love* them?"

"I suspect he might. I don't want to seem presumptuous by claiming to speak for God."

"You were presumptuous when you spoke *to* him," one woman said. Her voice had an edge to it. "Why could you presume to dictate how God ran Hell?"

Dayne felt the darkness of pain wash over her. They had to know, she supposed. So she told them. She told them about the old people on ventilators, about the feel of breaking bones beneath her hands, about the sound of shattering old ribs, so precisely like the sound of cracking knuckles. She told them about doctors who wouldn't give up, and people who couldn't die: nearly drowned children who would live for years without ever waking again, brain-dead husbands and wives whose families came daily to visit the empty husks of their loved ones' bodies—who came to see those visits as visits to a grave, while grief drained life and joy out of them. And she talked about Torry, whom she had loved and lost, and about the fate she feared had awaited him, and the pain she feared he suffered and did not want him to suffer. She talked about this as being pain greater than any she had ever seen, greater than anything she could comprehend.

"If my husband ran around on me, I'd *want* him to burn in Hell," one female reporter offered.

"Not if you love him," Dayne said. "Your own hurt is temporary. Hell's pain was eternal." She brightened. "But not now. Now there is hope even in Hell."

Chapter 24

Lucifer did not take kindly to Dayne's interference. Defections from Hell's ranks of suffering damnedsouls had been high before—people who discovered Hell was a real place were often quick to repent—but the news of Dayne's pointless, redundant do-gooder intervention had indeed spread hope even to the depths of the Pit, and numbers of repenters were surpassing numbers of new meat for the first time in millennia.

Lucifer drummed his talons on the red lacquer surface of his desk and glared. Agonostis was, as far as he could tell, approaching the matter of Dayne's damnation with intelligence and efficiency—and he was doing yeoman work setting up Hell's branch office upstairs, too.

But Lucifer wanted a fail-safe. He wasn't sure what form this fail-safe should take; however, he did have an idea of who ought to be given the job of backing up Agonostis.

He paged Pitchblende, and when the demon appeared, he said, "Find Jezerael and bring her here. I have an assignment for her."

When Jezerael arrived, Lucifer greeted her coldly. "Your enemy does well in his assignment on Earth."

Jezerael said nothing.

"I think he shall, if he succeeds in his work there, become my unquestioned second in command—and

I think you shall become his servant." Lucifer saw Jezerael's eyes turn vicious and hard. Still she said nothing; her control was superb. "I might offer you a chance to win the role I would give to him . . . if you dare take it."

"I'll take it," she snarled.

"Yes. I thought you would. If you would be my second, and have Agonostis as your slave, bring me the soul of Dayne Kuttner before Agonostis can get it. You'll go up to Earth, you'll follow the rules there. . . ."

"I thought the total number of Hellspawn who could go to the surface were already there."

"We have had one or two . . . little accidents. There are openings. I'll slide you into one of them." Lucifer shrugged. "You'll find yourself bound by the rules. You'll also still be responsible for improving the Lust and Fornication department—anything *you* personally do on the surface will count toward your numbers. You can't count the other Hellspawn's activities, I'm afraid. Agonostis will get all the credit for that."

"I don't care. I can make it work. And I can get Dayne Kuttner's soul, too."

"Let's hope so. Things will be quite unpleasant for you if you don't—Agonostis will surely see to that. You have an hour to prepare. Make the most of your time."

Chapter 25

Jezerael studied the computerized notes about Dayne Kuttner and compared them with details about Agonostis' movements. She read the bio in slow-time, went over informed speculation about why Dayne had made the prayer she had . . . and then she looked with careful attention to detail at Lucifer's annotations on the spy's reports of her archenemy's approach to the problem of Dayne Kuttner.

She began to laugh. "The stupid bastard is trying to damn her with lust . . . with *lust*! She went without sex from the day her husband died until the present, and it would be obvious to anyone but a moron that she simply hasn't wanted to debauch herself—she's had as many opportunities as anyone could." Jezerael leaned back in her chair and smiled slyly. "I can see now that it's definitely possible to stay too long in one job, and think the familiar solutions are the only solutions that can work. Lucky for me I'm broader in thought and clearer in sight than that."

Jezerael had to admit that Dayne was showing interest in Agonostis' cover persona. It wasn't the sort of interest that was going to land Dayne in Hell—at least Jezerael didn't think it was, but she thought she would be wise to destroy any chance Agonostis had of finessing Dayne into the corral. Timing would be very important; she'd have to find a moment that would leave Dayne feeling totally hurt and betrayed. She smiled as the perfect scenario occurred to her. She'd have to see about getting a reliable spy of her own, so she could keep tabs on Dayne and Agonostis; if he was any damned good at his job at all, Jezerael's moment would come.

And then she needed to devise her own plan of seduction.

She didn't know what that would be yet . . . but it would be something Dayne would find irresistible.

Chapter 26

"Dayne!" A tall, dark-haired form pushed his way through the crowd, and resolved into Adam.

Dayne waved, and watched as the camera lenses turned to focus on Adam, and noted the curiosity and calculation in the eyes of the reporters. She could see them formulating their questions as he approached.

She was tired. She didn't want to answer any more questions. She'd been sitting on the brick and concrete of her front steps as long as she could stand. She wanted to be up and moving, she wanted to be someplace quiet and secluded; she didn't want to see anyone else with a picket sign or a T-shirt with her face on it.

Adam blew by the waiting reporters with a cold, experienced "no comment," and hurried to her side. He whispered in her ear, "I have my car parked one street over. Do you want to get out of here?"

"More than anything," she told him.

He smiled. "You any good at running?"

"I'm fairly fast and I have lots and lots of stamina."

"That will do." He took her hand and leaned down to whisper in her ear, "Be ready to make a break for it."

She nodded solemnly, and stood.

"That's all, people. Go home. She doesn't want to talk anymore."

The reporters protested, demanding to know who Adam was and what right he had to chase them away. Behind them, a faint, unhappy rumble rose from the crowd. Dayne had been so reasonable and so open, they seemed to feel they were entitled to keep her talking indefinitely.

Adam started leading her away, across the yard, toward the back of the apartment and the opposite street. The reporters, losing their fear and their manners in the same instant, shoved in on her and began shouting last-minute questions and crowding in.

"Who's your boyfriend?"

"What do you have to say to the people who claim you're really a Satanist, and that when you prayed, you prayed to the Devil?"

"Why didn't you pray for something useful, like world peace or enough food for everyone!"

"Run," Adam shouted.

They ran—Dayne had been perfectly honest in her assessment of both her speed and her endurance. Long-legged Adam kept pace with her with difficulty, while the encumbered cameramen and their reporter cronies were left in the dust.

"Turn right," Adam gasped, while the mob trailed behind them.

Dayne gathered herself and sailed over a low holly hedge—the gleaming, spear-edged leaves were encouragement to keep her legs high in classic hurdler's form. Adam took the hedge without difficulty. Both of them picked up speed when they encountered a Rottweiler on a chain considerably longer than either of them had guessed. A chain-link fence proved an obstacle, until Adam lifted Dayne over—after she was safely on the other side, he rested one hand on the top of the fence and vaulted over it, and she thought perhaps she ought to hate him. But she didn't.

"How much farther?"

He was breathing hard. "The corner. Up there."

The corner was another chain-link fence and a good two holly hedges away. She saw some of the reporters and cameramen splitting off in a clear flanking maneuver, and pointed that out to Adam as they ran.

"Still have. Your pepper gas?"

"Sure."

"Pull it out. Hold in your. Hand."

They were at the second fence. He lifted her over. She pulled out the pepper gas canister and held it up.

The flanking reporters stopped, and the cameramen decided suddenly to take their pictures standing still.

"Good job." Neither holly hedge was too terrible, though Dayne thought the people on the corner were being a bit slack in their trimming. Still, she and Adam arrived at the car intact and laughing. He opened the door for her, she jumped in, and they zoomed out of the side street, across a main boulevard, down another side street, and then another, and finally they were out of the dreadful traffic that had inundated her neighborhood, and away from people who knew who she was.

It was only then that she realized she was driving to an unspecified destination with a man she didn't know at all. He seemed so warm and familiar, and that friendly face in the middle of the swarm of reporters had been like a beacon of light. But she wasn't comfortable with the situation—as much as she liked Adam, she didn't know him enough to trust him. Her right hand slid into her jacket pocket, and held the pepper gas. Insurance.

"I saw you on the television," he said. He took a corner a bit clumsily, and Dayne was startled when she realized he didn't drive very well. He had a problem with his clutch, and had to look at the stick when he shifted gears. He seemed unaware of her scrutiny. "You looked good," he told her. "But you also looked like someone who could use an excuse for an escape."

"I was getting tired of answering the same questions in different ways," she agreed.

"You were very nice to them." He looked left and right, started to turn left, and muttered, "Damn. One way street."

"Charlotte's full of them," she told him. "I was afraid the mob would stone me if I didn't explain things to them."

Adam laughed. "After last night? If you'd told 'em to kiss the ground you walked on, they would have."

"Last night?"

"When you took apart the local reporter—you didn't know they ran that clip on CNN?"

Dayne smiled a toothy smile. "I figured they must have run it somewhere—the male reporters today were all standing around with their ankles crossed."

"Probably wore athletic cups to the interview, too." Adam sighed. "Look, I had intended to ask you out, and have both of us meet at a nice restaurant— something that would give you a chance to get to know me. I never intended to shanghai you, but you really did look like you needed a rescue. And since we're here, why don't you let me buy lunch? Have you had anything to eat?"

Dayne pressed her hands to her face. "My lunch! I left it on my step when we ran off." She shook her head. "No, I haven't had anything." She thought of her lunch sitting on her landing, then considered how she must have looked, running across yards and jumping fences. She sighed.

"What's wrong?" Adam's look of concern did a lot to reassure her.

"I don't know that running was the best thing to do.

I'm afraid it will make them think I have something to hide."

"You don't?"

She looked at him sidelong, and he shrugged. "Sorry. Everyone I have ever known has had *something* to hide. But I've never known anyone like you before. The fact that you were the person who got the Hellspawn paroled to Earth came as quite a shock." He turned again, this time grinding the gears badly before he got the clutch all the way in. He sighed and muttered, "These things always look so easy when somebody else drives them." Then he pulled over into a parking lot and put the car into neutral. While it idled, he turned to face her and said, "Of course running was the right thing to do. Dayne, if you'd stayed there being polite to them, they would have kept throwing questions at you until you fell down from exhaustion. They don't care that you kindly sat and answered every question you were asked. They use people. They're looking for the sensational, and if you're reasonable with them, they'll keep prodding you until you do something sensational. They didn't want to hear you telling them about things that mattered to you. They just wanted pictures of screaming picketers and riots in the street."

"Oh."

"The station I was watching gave you pretty good coverage, but I flipped around a little—most of the other stations had experts in, who were commenting on what you had to say, and explaining why you were wrong."

Dayne looked at him, startled. "Why I was wrong?"

He nodded. "Their expert commentators, ministers mostly, were explaining how what you had asked of God was counter to the Bible, or how your theology was wrong, or how God didn't perform miracles anymore so the fact that the Hellspawn were here could not have been an act of God. The majority of the people listening to your interview only heard little sound bites taken from the things you said, as often as not taken out of context, and always heavily edited and explained by the commentators."

"So I was wasting my time?"

"*They* were wasting your time. Give credit where it's due. You were doing the best you could. They weren't."

Dayne leaned back into the bucket seat and closed her eyes. "I wonder what they'll come away thinking."

"Whatever they thought before." Adam took a deep breath and put the car into reverse. He backed up in the parking lot, fought with the gears, and got the car rolling forward toward the street again. "Anyway, how about something to eat. I'll buy, by way of apology for dragging you away from your press conference in such an undignified manner. You, however, will have to pick out the restaurant—I've been working nearly around the clock since I got here, and haven't had the time to explore."

Dayne opened her eyes and looked around—she was no longer sure where she was. Charlotte was a big enough city that even people who had lived in it most of their lives could find places to get lost. Dayne, who had moved to Charlotte to be with Torry, and who had stayed because she had an apartment and work, had explored only the parts she needed to, and had avoided the rest.

"I don't know. This isn't my part of town."

"How about an adventure, then?"

She tilted her head and gave him a little half-smile. "Just what I need—another adventure." Then she laughed. "Why not? What sort of adventure did you have in mind?"

"Stop at the first place we come to and eat there?"

Dayne looked around the neighborhood and winced.

"Um . . . maybe we'd better drive a bit further first. I don't like the look of this neighborhood." Streetwalkers sauntered along the sidewalk in broad daylight—absolutely gorgeous women in awful clothes, and young boys wearing lipstick, and little girls with high heels and hard eyes. She wondered at them . . . so many congregated so close together. They seemed to be doing a brisk business, though.

Adam looked at the street and nodded thoughtfully. "Yes. I do think you're right. So let's not be *that* adventurous. I vote for cowardice and a bit more driving."

Dayne laughed. "Second the motion and call the question."

Adam said, "All in favor?"

"Aye!" they said in unison.

They continued to drive with Adam apparently picking the streets at random, and suddenly Dayne recognized the neighborhood. She'd never come at it that way—her own route stuck to major arteries and skipped the red-light district—but first houses and yards and then everything became recognizable.

"Yes!" she said. "There are several restaurants down that way."

Chapter 27

Jezerael arrived precisely where she wished to be—inside a shopping mall restroom—wearing one suit of Hellwear, and carrying a huge amount of cash and a large leather backpack full of maps and information. She strolled out of the restroom, picked an expensive women's boutique, walked through the doors and said, "Outfit me. I need everything, and I want everything top of the line." After a suitable tip, the two women who ran the boutique were more than happy to close up for the rest of the day and give her their complete attention. They were equally happy to recommend a hairdresser, and set up an immediate appointment for her, and to call a cab to get her there.

Because Jezerael had never been human, she had never known the sort of pampering money could buy. She hadn't gotten it in Heaven, and certainly not in Hell. She liked it—liked it enough that she thought she would rather stay in North Carolina than return to Hell. Even if Lucifer offered her a promotion. She decided she wanted Agonostis' Earthside job. He could take back Lust and Fornication—hell, he could have Plagues and Diseases for that matter. Although it would please her much more if he ended up as a damnedsoul screaming in the Pit.

So there was another goal. Stay on Earth. See

Agonostis fry. Throw Dayne Kuttner to Lucifer and his dogs.

The woman cutting her hair said, "So what do you do?"

"Disease research," Jezerael said before she'd had a chance to think about it.

"Oh, my." The plump little bleached blonde looked impressed. "Are you a doctor?"

Jezerael wrinkled her nose. "No. A scientist."

"You have the strongest nails I think I've ever worked on," the girl doing her manicure said. "And they're so long."

You should have seen them before, the fallen angel thought. They could rip out a liver with one swipe— very convenient when doing biopsies. She didn't say any of that, of course. It might be amusing to assume her true form in front of these pitiful mortals, but if she did, she'd get a lousy haircut, and her nails would have to be re-done.

"So . . . do you think the light red . . . or the clear?"

Jezerael looked at the two nail polish shades the girl held up for her approval, and said, "Neither. I want a dark red. Something . . . dangerous."

Both women tittered. "Hot date, huh?"

Jezerael smiled slowly and said, "Those are the only kind, aren't they?"

Both women laughed and agreed that they were. The topic of conversation drifted, and settled back into what had been the day's major groove—Hell in North Carolina.

"Did you know Sadie Pickers and her husband put their house up for sale?" the cosmetologist asked the manicurist.

"You're kidding! They'd have to be crazy. Nobody's going to buy a house in North Carolina now. My husband said we ought to put the wheels back on our trailer and drag it on up to Virginia, and I'll tell you what—I never thought I was going to be grateful we lived in a trailer, but I am now."

"Don't tell me you're going to move."

"I reckon we are. His family is real religious, and they don't like the idea of sharing the state with Hell."

The cosmetologist said, "I guess if we could get anybody to buy the farm, we'd probably move. . . ." She sighed. "I don't know, though. That farm's been in our family for nigh onto a hundred and fifty years. I don't know that I'd want to see it go into somebody else's hands."

"But what about those devils and all?" The manicurist frowned and shook her head.

"I kind of figure it all depends on why God put 'em here. Maybe that little nurse was right, and they're here so we can help 'em find Heaven."

"Well, that devil last night said they were here to corrupt us and drag us all down to Hell."

"Shirley, I'll tell you what. I don't figure they can do anything to us now they weren't doing before—only now we can see them and catch them at it. And we know they're real for sure now, so we have every reason to live straight and treat each other right."

Jezerael smiled up at the cosmetologist. "Lucky for the Hellraised not everyone is as sensible as you, or Hell would be an empty place."

When they were finished, she looked stunning. What's more, she'd successfully passed as human, and she'd had a chance to listen in on real humans up close.

The cosmetologist had been right for the most part. Humans who knew what she was would avoid her seductions—and the doom of Hell—unless what she offered was something a fallen angel could offer, but a human could not. She did not know yet what she could offer Dayne Kuttner, either as a human or an

angel, that Dayne would willingly sell her soul for—
but she would find something. There was always
something.

Every human had one impossible dream. She had a
bit less than a month to find Dayne's.

Chapter 28

Dayne and Adam went down the menu, not certain about anything. Their waiter arrived with a list of the afternoon specials. Dayne decided on the clam and corn chowder for an appetizer, fresh blackened trout, and stuffed potato.

Adam smiled and said, "Yes. That's exactly right. I'll have the same."

It would be very easy to love a man like him, Dayne thought.

The waiter brought their drinks and vanished again. Dayne sipped hers and said, "So if you hate computers, how in the world did you end up with the job you have?"

Adam laughed. "I just sort of fell into it." He seemed to find the remark very funny, though Dayne didn't get the joke. Adam took a little sip of the Coke, nearly choked, and said, "That's . . . . sweet!" He wrinkled his nose, then pushed the drink back. "Seriously, I was second-in-command at the main corporation, but this incredible new opportunity opened up. If I can make a go of it, North Carolina could give us a base of operations like we've never had before. The growth potential here is just beyond belief. So I ended up with sort of a lateral promotion. . . . I'm in charge of the North Carolina operation, but the boss is still watching every move I make. If we can't make a go of this" —he drew his finger across his throat and made a cutting sound— "I'm in hot water." He shrugged. "It's no big deal, though. If I weren't damned good at what I do, I would never have made it this high. I'll win . . . and we'll be one hell of a success."

Dayne chuckled. She enjoyed talking to people who enjoyed their work. "It sounds fun."

He gave her a broad, slightly wicked smile. "It's very competitive. There are at least a dozen other department heads who would do anything to get my job . . . well, my main job. This North Carolina move will only be something everyone else wants if I can get it to go. If I fail at it, then it's going to become the post that the big boss uses to punish screw-ups. So a lot is riding on it."

"You sound like you enjoy the challenge."

"I had my doubts when I got the assignment. The boss gave me a lot of stipulations, and he wants the operation in the black and self-supporting inside of one year."

"I don't have much to do with major corporations, but that seems like a pretty steep order."

Adam nodded. "It is. I think I can do it, though."

"I'll bet you can. I bet you'll be great." She sighed. "I need a break from what I'm doing. You guys ever need nurses?"

"We have some medical interests. In fact, maybe I can bring over an application, and even get you an interview. I don't have anything to do with the medical subdivision of the corporation, but I know who does. I'd get a few points for recruiting you, though; we can always use new people, and Satco is definitely an equal-opportunity employer."

"Satco?"

He put a hand over his mouth. "You didn't hear that. The corporation is keeping a low profile for now."

She smiled. "Hear what?"

He shook his head ruefully. "Thanks. But I didn't want to monopolize the conversation. You're a nurse. Do you like it? I heard a little bit about it in your interview—it sounded pretty grim to me."

Dayne shrugged. "There are transcendent moments when I know I've done something that mattered—there have been a few in the years I've been doing this when I've known I was the only person who could have done what I did. Doing the kind of nursing I do, I have to live for those moments, because the rest of my work is so grim." The food arrived, and she dug into hers. "I love my patients. I got into nursing because I wanted to help people, and my patients are all I could have ever hoped for. I hate the paperwork I have to do because it keeps me away from them. I don't care much for Administration, because they focus on the bottom line—which is invariably monetary—and sometimes that focus interferes with good patient care. I get along pretty well with most of the doctors, but there are a few I wish would go away."

Adam nodded. "The ones who keep your patients, who have no hope, hanging on."

"Those are the ones. How did you—?"

"That was the part of the interview I caught. You're an interesting woman." He lifted an eyebrow. "Challenging, even."

They talked about inconsequential things for the rest of the meal. The waiter returned to offer dessert.

"The hot apple pie with vanilla ice cream," she told him. "Ice cream on the side, please."

The waiter nodded. "And you, sir?"

Adam looked at the dessert menu. "Devil's Food Fudge Tower." He winked at Dayne.

"Yes, sir. That's been very popular tonight," the waiter said with a straight face. The waiter shook his head. "From the news, you would think they were everywhere, but I don't know *anyone* who's seen them. I would almost think this was a prank like that Orson Welles radio show I heard about, where everyone thought the Martians were coming . . . but I don't suppose there would be any way to get all the networks involved in something like that."

"You wouldn't think so," Adam said. "I haven't seen any of the Hellraised. How about you, Dayne?"

She shook her head. "You know, I would have thought I, more than anyone else, would have at least seen some of them by now."

"Stopping by to thank you?" Adam asked. "Yes. I suppose you have every right to think that. . . ."

Dayne shook her head vigorously. "Gratitude wasn't what I expected at all. If anything, I would have anticipated a fair amount of trouble from them. Temptation, you know. The trials of Job. Something like that."

She couldn't understand Adam's reaction. He looked . . . shaken. "You *expected* to be tempted?"

She didn't think she was imagining the fact that he'd gotten paler, either. "Adam . . . are you all right?"

Whatever the strange reaction was, it passed. "Sure. But, I don't know—I guess if I were you I would have expected gratitude from Hell and a certain amount of protection from Heaven. I mean, you're evidently something pretty special."

"Not only do I not expect gratitude from Hell, but I even doubt that many of Hell's Fallen will take this opportunity that they've been given. I suspect most of them will choose to stay in Hell."

Adam looked bothered. "Why would you think a thing like that? Everybody wants second chances."

She chuckled. "But almost nobody is mature enough to admit he was wrong and apologize for what he did . . . and really mean it. I think Lucifer's biggest problem is being too stubborn and too immature to admit he screwed up." The apple pie arrived, ice cream in a separate dish; she took a bite and sighed. "Perfect," she told the waiter. "Absolutely perfect." The waiter smiled and put down Adam's dish, mounded high with layers of cake and ice cream and fudge and chocolate chunks, then vanished again, in the manner of all superior waiters. Dayne gave Adam a wicked grin. "Not that I know Lucifer, of course."

Adam said, "I imagine by this time he knows you."

She nodded. "I'm sure. And I'm sure sooner or later he'll send one of his loyal fiends after me."

"You don't seemed worried by that."

She stopped and thought about it. "I suppose I'm not, really. God never lets us carry more of a burden than we can. Besides," she arched an eyebrow at him and said with a perfectly straight face, "if some devil gives me trouble, I'll just ask God to turn him into a puddle on the ground."

Adam swallowed and nodded slowly. "I figured it would be something like that."

Chapter 29

"I'll just ask God to turn him into a puddle on the ground." Agonostis snarled and slammed his fist into the horn; the car blared at a lady sitting in front of him who hadn't been doing anything wrong. The light was still red. Agonostis didn't care. He laid on the horn again.

He'd been driving around ever since he had dropped Dayne off at her apartment, trying to think of some way to shatter her faith. She liked him; he knew she liked him. She wanted him—of course. What woman wouldn't? He knew how to play the game—he could make himself into the man of every woman's dreams (or the woman of every woman's dreams, for that matter, but he preferred the state of maleness). Nice girls had to be played differently than sluts—different bait for different fish, he thought. For a nice girl, he had to give every appearance of taking his time, of being interested in her as a person, in wanting to spend time with her that wasn't related to sex. He knew he was playing Dayne right. He'd gotten the conversation back on track, and made a date with her for the next evening . . . and when he had, he'd seen her whole face light up. He had her, dammit. She wanted him.

But could he make her want him enough to sell her soul for him? He'd been sure before, but now he had his doubts.

Just getting her into bed wouldn't count. That wasn't a Hellfire offense. He wished it were—he would have had numbers beyond belief if he'd gotten two souls every time two people who weren't married got laid. It was their *intent*. . . .

He doubted he could get her to try to get knocked up just to get him to marry her. *That* was a damnable sin, but she didn't seem to be enough of a liar or a cheat to pull that stunt. He didn't think he'd have any luck getting her to sleep around on him—over years, with sufficient neglect and bad treatment, maybe, but that was one of those mitigating circumstances that could sometimes go the other way. It tended to be forgivable. And as for getting her to sleep with him, then cheat on him in less than a month—not a chance.

He drove, and glowered, and sulked, and drove some more.

"She's really something, isn't she, O Perfidious One?"

Agonostis jumped. When he was alone, he preferred to stay alone. He snapped, "What are you doing here, Earwax? You're supposed to be spying on her."

"Your car phone is about to ring. I'm going to answer it for you."

"Do and die."

"But I like answering phones. I was going to do Walter Cronkite—"

The phone rang. Earwax made a stab for it, but Agonostis got it. "What?"

"Wrong answer." Lucifer's voice cut through Agonostis' reverie.

"My apologies, lord and master," Agonostis said, and hoped he sounded both sufficiently obsequious and sufficiently soothing. "I expected the call of an underling . . . since you don't need phones."

"I don't like for you to get too settled." Lucifer laughed, and Agonostis' stomach lurched. The human body, he thought, was much more prone to those physical expressions of terror. It was annoying. "I don't think I have to worry about it, though," the Archfiend said. "I expect you'll be down here in a month, trying out life as an imp. That will be so entertaining."

"I'll get her," Agonostis said. He sounded confident enough—he wished he felt so confident. "I have some plans for expanding our North Carolina operations, too. I suspect with good management and persistence, we can affect the whole of the world from right here."

There was a pause. "I saw your plans. Well thought-out. I won't finance you, of course. I'll expect you to achieve that set-up on your own revenues."

"I already anticipated that . . . sir."

"It's ambitious, I grant you." He realized that Lucifer begrudged him the idea—its cleverness utilized modern technology and modern interests and rang some new changes on some very old sins. The Lord of Evil didn't keep up on modern technology—he'd picked up the last of his really vile new ideas from monks during the Spanish Inquisition. "I'm sure your successor will find the plan quite a challenge to implement."

"I'll get her soul," Agonostis snarled. "If I can't get her to turn her back on God on her own, I'll leverage her—I'll use her friends or her family. Or maybe even old Torry. I assume we still have him."

Agonostis glared at the telephone and told Lucifer, "She'll curse God. Before I'm through with her, she'll curse God and Heaven and the day she was born."

Chapter 30

"It's certainly an *interesting* experiment, sir," the angel said. God, in the Event Room to check on progress, had asked for an opinion. God liked to get opinions, but the angel didn't like to give them.

The two of them watched the enormous bank of monitors that scanned the activities and points of interest in North Carolina. The views of Lucifer's legions racing around causing trouble in all sorts of ways was fascinating—just as the aftermaths of earthquakes, hurricanes and bad train wrecks could be fascinating.

God raised an eyebrow and smiled slyly. "Oh, come now. Just 'interesting'? You can say more than that."

But I'm not sure that I should, the angel thought. However, what God asked for, God got. "I simply wonder why you would choose to reveal yourself after all the trouble you've taken to hide the obvious signs of your handiwork. If you value both belief and your people's free choice, why reveal yourself now?"

God chuckled. "I suspected that had crossed your mind."

He didn't say anything else, and the angel looked at him expectantly.

"You want my reasons?"

The angel nodded. "If you don't mind."

God said, "You assume humanity will take the existence of Hell as proof of the existence of Heaven."

The angel nodded.

"That would be a logical assumption—but humans are anything but logical, and belief is not a thing that can be reached by logic anyway. They see proof of Hell, and so a good many of them will believe in Hell. In evil."

"Not all?"

"Certainly not. If there are people who believe, in spite of all evidence, that the world is flat or that televangelists work for me, there will be people who believe, in spite of all evidence, that Hell really isn't there."

"What about the rest?"

God sighed. "Some will believe, of course. But some won't. When they see proof of evil, but no obvious signs of counteracting good, what then will force them to believe in Heaven? In any case, evil is so much easier to believe in than good, for it is so much easier to do and to see."

"You don't think you've . . . er . . . stacked the deck, then?"

God laughed outright. "Anaraphel—I always stack the deck! I play to win—and I can only win when every soul I have created is fulfilled and challenged and joyous. That's my game . . . my goal. But to use your metaphor, I've decided to play a different variation for a while."

Chapter 31

No one said anything to her when she got to work, but Dayne found prayer requests on her locker when she walked into the nurses' lounge. There were a lot of them—layers of little yellow stick-up notes placed row over curling paper row, so that her locker looked like Big Bird. People wanted new cars, or money to pay off their mortgages, or to win the Publisher's Clearinghouse sweepstakes. They wanted to find someone who would love them; they wanted their divorce settlements to work out. They wanted their elderly mothers healed of strokes, or their children healed of diabetes.

Dayne stared at the pieces of paper fluttering every time the door to the lounge opened and closed—little yellow squares carrying other people's pain and hope. She took them down and put them in her purse, aware of her colleagues' furtive glances.

They had missed the point—missed it entirely. They didn't see in her prayer the proof that their own prayers could be heard and answered; all they saw was that God had listened to her once, and so he surely would again. She'd given them hope . . . but it was the wrong kind of hope. They thought she could say a prayer and everything would be all right. They thought she could do miracles. She wondered what their reactions would be when they discovered that she couldn't.

She stopped by the supply cart and filled her pockets with tape and alcohol wipes and headed in to get report. Mary Deiner was already there, and Trish VanDyke, and Sally Reuters. The bleary-eyed night shift nurses were finishing up their last-minute charting, except for Frank Dorris, the nurse who was waiting to report.

He smiled when he saw her; he'd had the same patients during the night Dayne would have during the day, so he would report to her.

"Mrs. Paulley died at three thirty-five this morning," he said. "Bastard was in there coding her from about one a.m. He finally conceded defeat, but when you call him for anything today, watch out."

Dayne nodded. Dr. Batskold after he "lost" would be mean and sarcastic and vicious for several days. "Maybe I won't have to call him for anything."

Frank tapped the chart in his hand. "Well . . . don't count on your luck holding. At four-thirty a.m. I admitted Mr. Wilthom Fields, fifty-seven-year-old white male patient of Dr. Batskold, with chest pain—also hallucinations, paranoia, and possible psychosis." Frank went through Mr. Fields' vital signs on admission. "He's a twenty-four hour observation; his tentative diagnosis, aside from being nuts, is angina, possible myocardial infarction." Frank shook his head. "I don't think he's had a heart attack, though. I think he's cra-a-a-azy. He'll be out of here and on his way to Dorothea Dix tomorrow.

"Petters in E transferred out of the unit yesterday. In E today you have Mr. Walter 'Call Me Walt' Harvey." Frank grinned. "He's a nice old guy—seventy-five years old, patient of Dr. Weist, in to get a permanent pacemaker inserted. He's had some slowdowns during the night, but the temporary pacemaker kicked right in. He's prepped for surgery, and scheduled first—he may already be on his way by the time we get out of here. So you won't really have any orders on him until he gets back."

Dayne heard yelling and swearing from the patient rooms and frowned.

Frank said, "That's Fields. He's been doing that all night. Our only orders on him are cardiac—when I called to see about giving him a sleeping pill, Dr. Batskold said he wouldn't order anything for him because he didn't want to mask symptoms."

"So you listened to that all night." Dayne made a sympathetic face.

"Yep. Mostly he's been pretty funny. He says these little clear men keep stealing his covers and messing with the equipment. Every time we go in the room, the covers are in a pile on the floor in the far corner, and all of his equipment is bollixed up." Frank sighed. "It would be hilarious if he didn't insist on yelling at his hallucinations."

"Clear men, huh? That sounds different." Dayne grinned. "Usually *they* can see them just fine—they always claim the problem is with us. So . . . has he had any chest pain since admission?"

"Nope. Just clear men stealing his covers."

"Okay." Dayne sighed and took Fields' chart from Frank, noting times the patient was due medications, checking for specific treatment orders, comparing the orders with the drug administration record, and scanning the vitals and nursing notes. Meanwhile another night nurse came in to give her report to her day relief.

Frank said, "You ready to go do rounds?"

She finished the quick look at the orders—she would go over them again once Frank was out the door—

and went with him to meet the patients and make sure their equipment was all functioning.

The patient in G had indeed already gone to surgery. Dayne introduced herself to his daughter, who was waiting and passing the time by gathering up a few of his things to take home with her, and then Dayne and Frank went in to meet Mr. Fields.

His blanket was in a pile under the window. As they walked into the room, he was shouting at the top of his lungs and fighting with his sheet—though Dayne noticed he was definitely winning.

"Good morning, Mr. Fields," Frank said. "This is your day nurse, Dayne Kuttner."

He looked up at her with harried eyes, and said, "Can you see them?"

Dayne looked at the way he clutched his sheet and twisted it in his hands, at the weariness in his expression, at the sweat that beaded his brow. She shook her head sadly. "No, Mr. Fields. I can't."

"Would you look? I haven't been able to sleep all night—they keep stealing my covers; little men that look like they're made of clear gelatin. And they laugh at me and call me names. . . ." He wiped a hand over his forehead and looked at her imploringly. "Please . . . look."

She nodded and gathered the sheet into her arms and looked down at the bed. "You see? Nothing there."

"I see," he said gloomily. "But they'll be back as soon as you leave."

Frank said, "I'm going to go out and make sure I didn't miss anything. Catch up with me before I leave, okay?"

Dayne nodded. "I'll be out in a few minutes. I'm just going to fix his bed for him." As soon as Frank was out of earshot, she turned to her patient and said, "Guys never can get this right." She grinned at him, and with brisk movements, tied both the bottom of the sheet and the bottom of the blanket to the bed. She found a couple of safety pins and pinned the covers to the bed from under the sheet—then, for good measure, pinned them to the mattress from outside. She said, "Now you can get some sleep, Mr. Fields. The covers won't go anywhere."

His smile held an element of doubt, but he nodded. "I hope you're right. I'm so tired, the world is spinning. If I don't sleep soon, I'm afraid I'm going to lose my mind."

Dayne tactfully kept her opinions on the state of his mind to herself, and with a wave, headed out of the room to find Frank.

He was waiting by the lockers. He raised an eyebrow as she approached. "I don't hear him yelling yet."

She winked. "Secret trick of the trade."

"You brought in sleeping pills from home and gave him one?"

"Tied his sheets to the bed and pinned them there."

He smacked his forehead with the flat of his hand and groaned. "Why didn't I think of that? If we put up with his screaming for the last two hours for nothing, I'm going to turn in my nursing license."

"Oh no you don't." Dayne laughed. "Judy would leave the unit short-staffed again, and I promised myself I wasn't working overtime this week."

"I hear you. So . . . heard you had an exciting weekend. Saw you on the news, too. Pretty wild stuff."

Dayne nodded. "You could say that."

"I wanted to ask you something. . . ."

Her heart sank. Here it comes, she thought. She watched him, holding her breath.

"Lacy's been trying to get pregnant for years now—we've been to all the specialists, and we've done all the treatments. Nothing worked, and we really can't afford to keep trying—" He looked at her, and his eyes wore desperation plainly. "There's a waiting list so long for adopting that when we went in, the social worker told me that by the time the list gets to us, I'll be too old for them to consider us."

He looked at her and she could see it in his eyes— the hope that she could work a miracle.

She wished she could.

"Could you . . . pray for us?" he asked her.

"Frank, I will—" his eyes lit up, and she wished they hadn't "—but you have to understand that God will listen to you praying for something that you want with all your heart, more than he will listen to me praying for something *for* you."

"But if you could get God to give all of Hell a second chance—"

"I believe Torry is—was—maybe still is in Hell. The thing I wanted most in the world was to know that he didn't have to suffer forever. I was afraid for everyone else who was there, too—because of this place. Because I could imagine how terrible forever could be." She rested a hand on Frank's shoulder. "But you and Lacy are the people who want a baby more than you want anything else. *You* need to pray."

"You think we haven't?" Frank's eyes narrowed.

Dayne sighed. "No. I'm sure you have. I don't know why God answers prayers the way he does."

"But you will ask for us?"

Dayne nodded. "I'll ask. Please understand that I can't promise anything."

Frank grinned. "I figure we have a better chance with you than with Social Services."

Chapter 32

Jezerael handed her references and credentials to the hospital administrator. "They're all in the folder," she told him, and crossed her legs, making sure her raw silk skirt rode up, and the little slit in the side fell open when she did.

His eyes followed the skirt's movement, then looked away, and he blinked nervously. He flipped through the folder, making an obvious effort not to look at her. "Very impressive," he said. "Harvard is a fine institution."

She smiled and said nothing.

"How long do you think your . . . ah . . . your project will last?"

"I anticipate a completion date of just under one month . . . but my plans might change." She licked her lips. "Tell me, Mr. Connelly, are you married?"

She saw his eyes flick to his wedding band, and shift left quickly. He was considering lying to her. "Well . . . yes," he said. "I am."

She pressed her index finger to her lips and sighed, and studied him sadly. "Oh," she said. "How . . . nice."

The eyes flicked to the ring again, and to her face, and she could see him composing the lie in the instant his mouth opened. "I wish it were," he said. "My wife . . . well," he looked down at the top of his desk. "I won't bother you with my problems. You're here to do

147

research, and the problems of a man old enough to be your father—"

"Hardly," she interrupted, with a lift of her brow. ". . . are not problems you'd be interested in."

She uncrossed her legs and leaned forward, knowing that when she did so the elegant V-neck of her silk business suit gaped open and exposed a tremendous amount of cleavage. She'd practiced that move in front of a mirror in her hotel room the night before, and had been pleased with the effect. "I *would* be interested, though," she told him. "Perhaps we could discuss it over . . . lunch?"

He flushed. *Good.* His thoughts were going in the right direction, then. "Perhaps we could."

She stood, making something of a production out of it. "I have some additional things I need to take care of today. But if you are agreeable, I'd like to begin my data collection tomorrow morning."

"That would be fine."

"And perhaps we could have lunch tomorrow at noon—to discuss further what I hope to accomplish and how the research might benefit your hospital." She tugged at the skirt, and watched his Adam's apple bob up and down. "If you'll notify the ICU that I'll be coming tomorrow, and that I'm to have access to the charts . . ."

"Of course." He stood and came around the desk to walk her to the door. She held out her hand to shake, and when he took her hand, she caressed his palm with her thumb. He flushed, she smiled, and they stood staring into each other's eyes.

He cleared his throat.

She said, "I'll see you tomorrow, then, Mr. Connelly." She made her voice husky, a little deeper than it had been, slightly breathy.

"Wynne," he said. "You can call me Wynne . . . Dr. Jezick."

She regarded him through lowered lashes. "Wynne. I like that. And please call me Mhya."

She slipped away and sauntered out of the administrator's office, down the long, plush gray-carpeted hall, past several doctors, whose heads swiveled as she swung past.

He wasn't going to bother checking her references, she thought smugly. He had too much to lose.

Chapter 33

Mr. Fields snored—the snoring wasn't as loud as the yelling had been, but it was nonetheless impressive. Dayne grinned and glanced up at the monitor to check his heart rate. The green line that belonged to him wiggled across the screen in a perfect sinus rhythm, the heartbeat as normal as her own. The machine recorded him at eighteen breaths per minute, and she chuckled, marking down the number. She could double-check that from anywhere in the unit, simply by counting the number of times in a minute that she heard a musical whistle followed by a phlegmy rumble and punctuated with one sharp, short snort. Mr. Fields was to snoring what Paganini had been to the violin, or Rachmaninoff to the piano.

She looked up from the desk to study him through the glass. He looked fine, and quite content; he was curled on his side and sleeping soundly. She noted his condition, then frowned. When she'd looked up, she'd seen something—or rather, several somethings—that her mind hadn't registered at first.

She'd seen a quick flash of something that was the most astonishing shade of blue—and she had noted movement at the foot of Mr. Fields' bed. She looked up again, slowly.

She frowned. Whatever had been blue was gone.

However, the movement that had caught her attention remained quite visible. It appeared that someone was popping popcorn under Mr. Fields' blanket. Portions of the blanket at the foot of the bed bounced up and dropped down. Up and down. Up and down. Nothing came loose, because not even an act of Congress was going to get that blanket off the bed . . . but something was trying very hard.

Mary Deiner was charting next to her. Dayne nudged her with an elbow, and when Mary looked up, Dayne nodded in the direction of Fields' room.

Mary looked, and her mouth fell open and her eyes went round. "What in the world . . . ?"

"I don't know. I'm going to find out, though. Want to come with me?"

Mary nodded.

Both nurses dropped to a squat and used first the nursing station, then the half-wall below the glass in Mr. Fields' room for cover as they crept forward; they peeked through the glass into the room and watched, unmoving, as a little creature no more than two inches high, as transparent as if it had been molded of clear gelatin, scooted out from beneath the bedspread and dropped to the floor. Another of the little bouncing popcorn lumps stopped bouncing and wriggled to the edge of the bed, then slid out into view.

"He wasn't crazy," Dayne whispered.

"Or we are," Mary suggested.

"I want to catch one."

"Well, you're crazy, anyway," Mary told her. "The jury is still out on me."

"Help me—we have to see what they are."

"No we don't. We can just ignore them, and maybe they'll go away."

Dayne made a face at Mary. "I'm going to catch one."

"Fine. I'll be here to call for help if you run into

trouble." The other two ICU nurses had stopped in front of the nurses' station and were staring at Dayne and Mary. One started to say something, but Mary put a finger to her lips and shook her head. They shrugged and quietly moved into the nurses' station to watch monitors and to chart.

Dayne crouched just behind the doorframe and held her breath and listened.

An entire conference of the little gelatin-men was going on no more than two feet away from her on the other side of the wall—three out of every four words were hair-raising profanity, and she was the subject of their ire. It became obvious that they didn't think much of her trick with the sheets.

She was willing to bet they were going to think a lot less of what she planned to do next.

She jumped around the corner, landing in the middle of the confab and grabbing two; something crunched under her left knee, and suddenly it was wet and sticky, and she realized some of the tiny monsters had been closer than she thought. The two she captured shrieked like miniature banshees, and the rest, excluding the one ground into her uniform—she guessed there had been fifteen or so in all—blinked out of existence.

She held both of the little monsters by the scruffs of their necks and stared at them . . . and through them. They didn't feel at all the way she'd expected—she was reminded of the time she'd picked up a blue indigo snake as a child, expecting it to be slimy, and found instead that it was cool and dry and very firm and even pleasant to the touch.

The two little monsters were almost hot to the touch, and their skin was as hard and dry as a beetle carapace, with the same feeling of brittleness. Dayne had expected the little monsters to look almost identical, and was startled that except for the fact both were clear, they could easily have belonged to completely different species. One had a long tail and curling horns and a flat face. Spikes grew from the second monster's back; it was tailless and had a long-muzzled, reptilian face with two shorter spikes growing out of the tip of its nose. Both creatures had one head, two arms, two legs, tiny feet and tiny claw-tipped hands; both were unbelievably ugly, and both screamed imprecations at her at the tops of their lungs. They didn't bite or scratch, however—they just yelled. She held them firmly but gently, and looked down at the stain on her knee where the third little monster had been. She felt badly about that.

"Hush," she told both screamers. They didn't obey.

She started to head out of the room, holding her squirming prizes in front of her, when a light flickered in the air and grew into a tiny shimmering ball. She stopped, the tiny monsters shut up, and all three of them watched as a piece of paper grew inside the little ball of light. Then the light died and the paper hung unsupported in midair.

Dayne carefully transferred the monster in her right hand to her left, and with her free hand took the paper.

Hell's Accounting Department — Invoice

North Carolina Division of Bodies
Wastage and Destruction Sector
"We'll Have Our Pound Of Flesh"

INVOICE NO: 518KT34972-00000000014A

Bill To:
Dayne Kuttner
Earth Region 17945-8492-253
Sisters of Hope Hospital
Charlotte, North Carolina

Customer Status:
☑ New Customer
☐ Regular Client
☐ Account on Established Credit

Tracking Data: 15 BJRT	Invoice date: H.D.14/346/97084	Invoice Processor: Ulkbilge
	Customer Number: NC1487245	

QTY	DESCRIPTION	UNIT PRICE	AMOUNT
1	Gremlin 3rd Class, body, wasted and nonrecyclable—broken during unwarranted attack	$43.25	$43.25
1	Replacement body, Gremlin 3rd Class	$43.25	$43.25
1	Punitive damages for squishing one of God's little creatures	$462.81	$462.81
	SUBTOTAL		$549.31
	SALES TAX		$33.02
	SHIPPING & HANDLING		$18.00
	TOTAL DUE		$600.33

Cash or Hell-Card Only.
Bill due upon receipt—no grace period offered.
If you have any questions concerning this invoice, drop by our offices in Charlotte, Raleigh, Fayetteville, or our home office in Hell.
Pay promptly—interest is compounded daily on all overdue accounts.
Failure or refusal to pay is sufficient cause to change account status from new customer to regular client. For regular clients, we are always happy to open a Hell-Card ("Play Now, Pay Later") account.

Thank You for Your Business!

"Hell billed me?" she whispered.

The squished gremlin continued to stain the knee of her uniform, but another one appeared right in the spot where she'd landed. It swore at her, shook a tiny fist in her direction, and vanished into nothingness. She stood there for a moment, relieved that she hadn't actually killed the little creature, but at the same time furious about the bill. When at last she turned to go to the nurses' station, she caught another glimpse of that mysterious blue flash. When she turned to look, of course, nothing was there.

But something *had* been. She was certain of it.

At the nurses' station, Louise said, "Recovery just called with your pacemaker—he's been out of OR for an hour, but they said they're going to keep him for another hour. He isn't stabilizing the way they want." Dayne nodded. She put the bill from Hell down on the nurses' station and, with both howling, cursing gremlins still clutched firmly in one hand, she paged Dr. Batskold.

When he called, she was brusque. "I found out what Mr. Fields' problem was. I need you to come to ICU right away."

"I'm doing my charts in Medical Records. Can it wait?"

"No."

She heard an exasperated sigh, then she heard Dr. Batskold mutter, "They can never handle anything by themselves." One of the other doctors was evidently in the room, catching up on charts, too.

Dayne smiled grimly. She'd caught the little devils, but she wasn't going to try to figure out how to get rid of them. For another doctor she might have made the effort . . . but not for Batskold. For once, she regretted that she wasn't working the night shift; this would have been just thing to wake him up over at three A.M.

For that matter, she was more than a little curious to

see how Dr. Batskold was going to include gremlins in his diagnosis. She'd bet Gremlin Infestation wasn't a discharge diagnosis that Medicare, Medicaid, or Blue Cross/Blue Shield would be willing to pay for.

Batskold made it to the unit fast enough; Dayne uncharitably thought that he was probably hoping for another code, so that he could be the mighty hero fending off Death again.

She said, "Fields wasn't hallucinating."

"Don't say that you called me up here to tell me that. He *was* hallucinating. He claimed he was seeing little clear men—"

Dayne held up the gremlins, which had stopped screaming and were trying to wriggle free, and said, "I caught two of them. There were quite a few more."

Batskold backed up and stared at the creatures in her hands and paled. "Jesus," he whispered, "what are they?"

"Gremlins. From Hell."

His eyes narrowed. "Are they real, or is this some prank?"

"They're real, all right."

He held out a hand. "Let me see."

Dayne shrugged, and handed one to him. "Hang on to it."

"Let me see the other one, too."

She handed him the second gremlin as well.

"God, they're ugly." He held both of them right up to his face. One of them peed on him, a thin stream of clear water.

He yelled and smashed it onto the nurses' station, where it crunched, then slammed the other one down beside it. Wiping his hands on his pants, he said, "Little bastards."

Dayne yelped, "Don't smash them! They're expensive—"

He pointed a finger at her and glared. "*You* mind

your own business. It's all your fault the damned things are here."

New gremlins, identical to the old ones, reappeared next to their smashed bodies. Dr. Batskold glanced down, yelped and smashed them again. Dayne turned and walked away. She'd tried to tell him, but he wasn't listening to her any better than he ever did.

Certainly no more than five minutes later, as she was helping Mary pull one of her people up in bed, Batskold fell silent.

"Keep your arms crossed over your chest, Mrs. Williams," Dayne told the patient. "You don't have to help us."

"A tiny little thing like you isn't going to be able to move me." Mrs. Williams was pushing the two hundred fifty pound mark, and most times, she would have been right.

Dayne shrugged, though. "I lift weights," she said. "I'm a lot stronger than I look." She and Mary grabbed the draw sheet and counted to three—on three, they turned and stepped, and Mrs. Williams found herself again up at the top of the bed, where she belonged.

Mary looked toward the nurses' station. "It's awfully quiet out—"

"*Nine hundred and fifty-eight thousand dollars?!*" Dr. Batskold bellowed. "I'm not going to pay that! Jeeeee-*zus* Christ!" Dayne peeked out to find him standing right where he'd been before, back when he'd been busy smashing gremlins. He held a sheet of paper in his hand that looked a lot like the one she'd received, but with more sheets appended. A ring of gremlins stood around his feet, staring up at him. His face was red, his usually fashionable gray hair stuck out in all directions, and his eyes were about to bulge from his face.

Dayne shook her head. "Dr. Batskold just got his bill." She tried hard not to smile, but the corners of her mouth twitched up in spite of her intentions. She turned her back to the window so that he wouldn't see her laughing if he looked her way.

Mary said, "He's leaving." An instant later, she added, "Oh, my God. The gremlins are going with him."

Dayne couldn't resist. She turned to take a peek, and sure enough, Dr. Batskold, stomping furiously out of the ICU, was followed by a glistening train of gremlins that ranged from an inch to four or five inches tall—all of which trailed after him, mimicking every move he made.

All she could think was that gremlins couldn't have happened to a more deserving person.

Chapter 34

Dayne pulled a loaf of bread and some jelly out of the refrigerator—she was too tired to cook anything more demanding than toast. While the bread browned, she punched the answer button on her answering machine. She'd forgotten to check it on Sunday, and she had a huge number of messages waiting.

She fast-forwarded through all the ones with her supervisor's voice. That took care of most of them.

"Good Lord, Dayne," her mother said in stunned tones. "What have you gotten yourself into? Call home as soon as you get in."

Dayne frowned. She understood her mother being concerned about her link to the Hellraised . . . but her mother's message didn't really seem appropriate. Certainly her lawn was still covered by sightseers and T-shirt sellers and fundamentalist picketers, and the police parked next to her drive still kept her Satanist supporters and her Christian supporters from ripping each other to bits, but the reporters were gone—and she didn't feel that she'd gotten herself *into* anything.

The next call was a hang-up, as was the one after it. The one following that was from Paige, who cleared her throat a few times before stammering, "Um . . . this is-is-is . . . not an emergency or anything, so . . . um, why don't you call me back when you can?"

Paige sounded bizarre.

Dayne shook her head. The next voice on the machine was deep and sexy. "Dayne, this is Adam." He was chuckling, and his voice sounded more bemused than anything. "If it isn't too much trouble, I'd like to stop over and see you tonight. . . ." Dayne's pulse picked up. She'd thought about Adam on and off during the day while she was working. He was obviously interested in her, a fact she found more than a little bit surprising—but delightful. Adam was the first person since Torry to give her goosebumps and butterflies; better yet, with Adam, she didn't have the endless nagging feeling that he was trouble waiting to happen. That gut instinct about her dead husband, proven right in the end, had warned her away from a number of otherwise nice men since. Its absence felt like a green light to Dayne.

Adam left his phone number and asked Dayne to call him back as soon as she could. Then he added, "I like the message," and Dayne groaned.

Suddenly her mother's enigmatic message, and Paige's nervousness, became clear. Dayne had forgotten to warn her family and friends about the strip-search-and-read-'em-their-rights machine message she'd left for the obscene phone caller.

She rewound that message to get Adam's phone number, then forwarded to the next. "Dayne? We haven't heard from you . . . but maybe next weekend won't be such a good time to stop by." That was her brother—with all the excitement, she'd forgotten he and his wife were hoping to come by, and worse, she'd forgotten she was supposed to get the weekend off if she could.

The next message was a hang-up.

So was the next.

On the following one, she heard a long silence, then softly, the whispered word "bitch" before the phone on the other end slammed down.

Her stomach lurched. Maybe that will be the last time he calls, she hoped. Maybe now he'll go away.

She took a deep breath and glared at her hands until they quit shaking. Then she called her mother, and explained that everything was fine; she called her brother and promised to try to get at least one day of the next weekend off. She called Paige, and explained her phone message, and that she couldn't come by because she had a date.

Then she called Adam.

"Satco, Executive Suite, this is Gwendolyn speaking."

The voice was beyond sexy. Dayne stared at the telephone for an instant, unnerved, then said, "Uh, yes . . . this is Dayne Kuttner. I'm returning Adam D'Agonostis' call."

"Oh, wow," the voice on the other end said, and most of the sexiness—and a good part of the femaleness—disappeared in an instant. "*The* Dayne Kuttner?"

That change and that sudden enthusiasm was even more unnerving to Dayne. "I suppose so," she said, then followed up that vague admission with a question which she hoped would effectively change the subject. "Is Adam in?"

"Oh. Yes, of course." The voice returned to its original form, and its owner put Dayne on hold.

A moment later, Adam picked up. "Hi, there. That's some message on your machine."

"I've been getting unpleasant phone calls," Dayne told him. "I decided I didn't want to get any more of them."

"That ought to do it." Adam laughed. "You'll be lucky to get many calls at all. Anyway, are you going to be home tonight?"

"Yes. I'd love to have you over."

"Good. Oh, by the way, I have some terrific news for you."

He sounded so cheerful—she smiled and leaned against the wall. "Really? Terrific news would be nice."

"I'm glad. I found an opening with Satco for an RN—if you're interested, I'll bring over an application for you to fill out."

Dayne considered the possibility of doing something that wasn't related to the ICU, and her smile grew broader. "I'm interested," she said. "Bring it over. You can tell me what you know about the job when you get here."

She hung up the phone and stared out of her kitchen window, considering Adam and wondering at her reaction to him. She couldn't blame it on being alone for too long; if that were the case, she would have been drawn to someone else long before this. Dr. Weist, who was handsome and considerate and intelligent, had been politely hinting he'd like to take her out, and his was only the most recent in a line of offers. Nor could she fool herself into thinking that Adam was right for her in a way no one else to that point had been—she was pragmatic enough to admit she didn't know anything like enough about him.

She smiled ruefully and watched the birds pulling berries off the dogwood tree in the backyard. She was pragmatic, but not so pragmatic that she hadn't fallen foolishly in love with a stranger.

"It isn't love," she muttered—but it was. She'd been in love only once before; and that one time she had fallen in love, it had been like this. She met Torry, she fell in love before she even knew him. . . .

"And look where that got me."

There were times when she wished she could fast-forward her life and look back at it the way biographers did on their subjects' lives; the biographers could always see what each choice meant. They could always see, from their lofty height, where their subjects were getting it wrong. Dayne, down in the thick of her life, had gone badly wrong with Torry. Moreover, while she could not believe that Adam was another version of Torry, the depth of her emotions and their suddenness unnerved her. Somehow, she feared, she was once again about to get it wrong.

Porthos jumped onto the counter and stared past her, his fur standing straight up. He hissed, and she felt the hair on the back of her own neck raise—atavistic response. She looked where the cat was looking, and caught only the briefest of flashes of blue from something that was moving in the apartment's tiny laundry room. She rose slowly, looking for a weapon. The baseball bat still leaned against the kitchen door. She grabbed that and stalked forward, silent and scared. She heard nothing from the laundry room . . . but the sense of *presence* was unmistakable. Porthos maintained his vigil on the counter, unwilling to move closer.

She took a deep breath as she reached the partly open door—then she kicked it open and jumped in, screaming, slamming the bat down at the same time in a short, vicious arc. . . .

Onto nothing. The tiny laundry room had only one door—the one through which she had come. It had no window, neither cabinets nor cubbyholes. She opened both the washer—empty—and the dryer—one still-damp pair of jeans and a few pairs of white cotton underwear. The intruder had neither a place to hide, nor a place to flee, yet he was not there. Rationally, she knew she should take that as proof that she had seen nothing, and that Porthos had been hissing at a phantom of his own imagining. She would have been happy to be rational.

The stink of rotten eggs, however, hung in the air.

The doorbell rang, and she jumped. Porthos yowled and fled from the kitchen—she could hear him thundering up the stairs as she walked to the front door.

She peeked out; Adam waited on the landing, a vase full of painted daisies and baby's breath in one hand, a folder in the other. He was staring back at the picketers and the T-shirt vendors, and the decreased but still fairly heavy traffic.

She opened the door, and he jumped a little and turned to smile at her—and she was struck again by how perfect his handsomeness was, and by how hard her heart began to beat just looking at him.

"Come on in."

He stepped inside and nodded back at the watching crowd. "Wonder how long it will take until they get bored with that."

Dayne, who had signed a few autographs on her way in from work, and who found the people on her doorstep interesting, just shrugged. "Big news is good for seven days," she told him. "By that rule of thumb, they'll all get tired and find something else to interest them by this Friday." She grinned. "Until then, I have to confess I'm enjoying the notoriety. I've never had anyone ask me for my autograph before. That's fun."

He looked genuinely surprised. "People find amusement in the strangest ways," he said, more to himself than to her.

"Has anyone ever asked for *your* autograph?"

He stood, staring down at his feet, studying his shoes and nibbling the corner of his lip for a long time. "No," he told her at last. "No one ever has."

"Then you don't know. I don't think it's at all strange to enjoy it."

"I'm not likely to find out." He changed the subject. "I brought you some flowers." He handed her the vase; the daisies were beautiful, pink and red and yellow and pale blue with bright yellow centers. The baby's breath filled in around them like a lacy cloud. "I hope you like flowers."

She grinned up at him. "Of course." She reached up to take the vase with her free hand, and Adam suddenly glanced down.

"Expecting reporters? Or was that for me?"

She realized she was still toting the baseball bat around. "Oh . . . no. I just thought I . . ." She shook her head. She had no desire to tell Adam about the intruder she couldn't be sure she'd had. She didn't want to sound silly. "Nothing," she told him. "I've just been kind of cautious lately."

He smiled down at her. "Very sensible."

She sighed. "That's me. Sensible." Her sensible-ness wasn't the trait she hoped Adam would pick up on, but then, he wasn't likely to see her standing in her hall, clutching the baseball bat she'd hoped to brain some intruder with, and say, "How sexy of you." She was going to have to make a point of being sexy if she wanted him to see her that way.

She led him back to the kitchen, and while she gave the daisies some extra water, listened to him rustling through the contents of his folder. She heard one of her kitchen chairs scrape along the floor—sounded like the one against the far wall . . . the one that would make it easiest for him to watch her. His gaze was a physical itch between her shoulderblades, and she felt—with some annoyance—the heat that rose in her cheeks in response. She was twenty-eight—far too old to feel like some infatuated twelve-year-old.

She turned to carry the vase to the table, and found, as she'd suspected, that he was watching her; more nerve-wracking, that the expression on his face hinted at an attraction as complete as what she felt.

Then she looked at her kitchen table, and was amazed at the sheer number of papers he'd brought.

"That's a job application?" she asked, and put the flowers down, and drew up a chair at right angles from his.

"It's a lot of things. Job application, permission form for Satco to access your records and add copies to our permanent files, disclosure statement, contract, job description for your job—a few other things. Mostly it's just a lot of red tape before Satco can hire you; we deal with a number of secret and sensitive things, and we have to be sure that you won't divulge any of our trade secrets."

"Why the contract?"

Adam smiled. "Because I know you'll get the job if you apply for it, so I'm saving a couple of days this way. It's selfishness on my part, I suppose, but since I met you, I haven't been able to think of much else. I like the idea of you working with me—and the sooner, the better." He leaned forward and rested his chin in his cupped hands and smiled at her—a smile that gave her goosebumps.

"I like the idea of working with you, too—but would I be? You haven't told me anything about the job, other than that it's for a nurse. And how would a corporation use my ICU skills?"

He sighed. "My knowledge of what the job entails is pretty limited—it isn't within my specialty, which is running things. I can tell you a little bit about it; you'd be working with our disease researchers. One small subdivision of Satco is heavily invested in cures for the major communicable diseases—and that area is a special interest of mine, so I try to find the best people for it. It's a pity you aren't a computer specialist, though. We don't have too much trouble finding qualified medical personnel, but, oh, man, we have top-level computer jobs going begging. We need system designers, hardware gurus, software geniuses . . ." He shook his head and chuckled. "But that doesn't apply to you, of course."

"No. Sadly. I wasn't kidding when I said I hated computers." Dayne leaned back in the chair and closed her eyes, considering the job she might get. Communicable disease research—that sounded pretty terrific. That might take her away from dealing one-on-one with all the loss and suffering eating her alive in the ICU. She considered. Research—in her mind, that word conjured up pictures of white lab coats and long, empty, echoing halls, little beakers of colored liquids and Petri dishes full of things to be studied under a microscope. An ivory-tower atmosphere, people who walked slowly and talked softly, air kept cool and always smelling of antiseptic and chemicals.

Realistically, the job of a research nurse was probably as messy and cluttered as that of a unit nurse—as full of memos and meetings and paperwork, yellow stick-up notes and petty frustrations and pain-in-the-neck doctors with God complexes.

Maybe, though—maybe it would be further from the pain. Dayne desperately needed some distance.

"Yeah," she said, opening her eyes. "Research sounds good. Let me see the job description."

She went over it carefully—it entailed drawing blood, patient evaluation (which Satco euphemistically referred to as "client follow-up"), lots of record-keeping, drug administration and documentation, treatment application, physical therapy . . . a lot of the usual nursing things. Care plans, of course—she loathed care plans. Everyone required them, but as carried out, they were the most worthless pieces of paper in the chart. She'd waged a big battle to revamp care plans into a working document not too long ago, and gotten stomped for it. Administration liked their paper the way they liked it.

Maybe Satco was better.

She said, "Well, it's worth looking into, anyway."

His smile got bigger. "Good. I'm so glad you feel that way." He started shoving papers across to her. "These are the important documents. Your records release . . . permission for background check . . . job history . . . contract . . . we'll start you at $24.50 an hour, and you'll get a raise at the end of six weeks if you work out, and evaluations every six months. The job has no limits—you can work your way to the very top if you're ambitious. And here's the application. This is the most vital document of all, because the people who evaluate me cannot have any reason to think I showed favoritism in hiring you."

"Are you?" Dayne raised an eyebrow.

He laughed. "Of course I am . . . but I also think you'll do extraordinarily well at the job. You're qualified. I did some preliminary checking just to make sure of that—I don't want to jeopardize my own career. From what I've heard so far—" he looked into her eyes and took one of her hands in both of his, "—hiring you will be the best thing I've ever done for my career."

Dayne heard the slightest tremor in his voice as he said that—his intensity and his sincerity amazed her. How had she gotten so lucky, to meet someone like him? She dug through her purse and found a pen, and tried to fill out the first of the forms. . . .

"This pen won't write," she muttered. She made circles on a piece of scrap paper and it worked just fine, but when she tried the forms again, nothing happened.

He'd stood up and dug through his pockets—he came out with a thick, bright red fountain pen. "I forgot—Satco's legal papers are specially treated to withstand a lot of adverse conditions. It takes a special kind of ink to write on them."

She took his pen and got to work. The application was long and tedious. When she finished it, she went through the disclosure form word by word before signing it. It was also long and tedious—and done in very small print. She went through three other sets of papers, reading each—it seemed to her that the wording got stuffier and more obtuse and the print smaller with every document she worked through. And when she got to the contract, she groaned. She flipped through the pages, counting them. "There are more than twenty pages in this thing—and I don't suppose you brought a magnifying glass with you, did you?"

"No." He smiled wryly. "Home office likes to cover every eventuality in its contracts. If you don't feel like wading through that whole thing, I can go over the main points with you—and when you're actually on staff, you'll get an employee handbook that has exactly the same thing in it, but in readable print."

Dayne had been through too many long days, and she was tired. She'd never in her life signed something without reading every word of it first—but those twenty-plus pages of micro-printed bureaucratese defeated her. "That sounds like a good idea. Just hit the high points. I'll go over the rest of it in the handbook."

He nodded, took the contract back, and pointed to the first section. "Responsibilities—that was in your job description."

"Skip it."

He nodded. "Rights."

"Skip them, too. Every company says the same old things in the same boring ways."

"Okay. Grievance procedures."

"That's included in the *contract*?" Dayne shook her head in disbelief.

"*Everything* is included in the contract." Adam made a face. "Home office likes to make sure everything is in writing."

"Do you like working for them?"

"Of course I do."

"Have you ever had any problems with them?"

"Sure. You know of anyone who hasn't had any problems at work?"

"No. But you're still with them. They must have resolved things pretty well. You ever work for anyone else?"

He nodded and, oddly, his smile vanished. "Yeah. Ages ago. But I only had one other employer—and I'm with Satco now, which tells you everything important about that."

Dayne said, "I've had a couple of those, too. Tell you what." She took the contract back from him. "I'm too tired to go through this right now, and I want to spend some time with you. I'll get the gist of things from the employee handbook." She sighed. "Where do I sign?"

One of his eyebrows slid slowly up, then down again. He shrugged. "The last page. Sign it, date it, and write the time."

Obviously he'd never signed a contract he hadn't read. Well, neither had she, but there was a first time for everything. She turned to the last page. It had a box for a notary seal, and a section of control numbers along the top. In the center was a long block of legalese that said she stated that she had read the contents of the contract and understood them, and agreed to them. Then came the line for her signature, and the place for the date and time—and a line for the signature of the "duly authorized representative of Satco."

She pressed the heavy red fountain pen to the paper, and felt the sharp bite of pain in her thumb—and looked down at her own blood dripping onto the signature line of the contract.

"Damn," she muttered. She grabbed a paper towel to wipe up the blood; the coating on the paper repelled ink. She hoped it would repel blood . . . but it didn't.

Instead, it soaked it in, and capillary action drew it into a big, disgusting blot. "Damn, damn!" She sucked on her finger and stared at the mess.

"Just write through it," Adam told her. "I won't care."

But Dayne pulled the back sheet of the contract free, and muttered, "I would." She grabbed the sheet in both hands.

Adam yelled, "Don't—"

She ripped it in two.

"—tear it!"

The paper burst into flames and fell, burning, into Dayne's lap. She shrieked and jumped up; her chair fell over backward behind her. She patted at her stomach and thighs with her hands and ran for the sink—her blouse and jeans were smoking, though not burning. She sprayed water on herself with the sink hose, and with a hiss, the sparks burning in her clothes went out.

She turned to find Adam stepping on the last blazing scraps of paper.

He looked up at her and said, "Satco doesn't want its sensitive documents to end up in the shredder. The coating on the paper usually prevents that. Everybody in the company knows about it."

Dayne nodded, mute.

"I should have warned you beforehand . . . but it just never occurred to me that you might tear a sheet." He winced. "You're okay, aren't you?"

"Fine," she said. "A little singed, I think, and a lot shook up. And I'm not sure I want to work for a company that uses exploding paper for its legal documents."

"Oh, Dayne . . ." He looked at her woefully. "Please tell me you're joking. You wouldn't let a little thing like that stop you, would you?"

Feeling shaky inside, she said, "I'm joking . . . I think."

He looked at the stack of papers lying on the kitchen table. "I'll have to bring another contract around for you—in a day or so. The papers I have will allow me to start all the necessary background work." He stared off at nothing and murmured, "I'm forgetting something. I know I am." He snapped his fingers. "Right. You have to have bloodwork and a urine drug panel done before you can start to work. I'll have one of our lab guys draw it for you."

Dayne nodded. She was still upset, and Adam was babbling on like nothing had happened. His behavior was wrong—right at that moment, he didn't seem like the Adam she thought she knew.

Then he said, "But, hey—we'll worry about that another day. We both worked hard today. Let's relax and unwind."

They went into the living room and settled onto the couch. Dayne found the remote and flipped channels until Adam said, "That looks good." He'd picked a TBS movie—an old one that Dayne didn't recognize.

They settled back to watch it, and she rested her head on his shoulder. She felt him stiffen the tiniest bit, then relax again. Then, tentatively, he put an arm around her shoulder. He felt warm and strong, he smelled nice, and Dayne relished the feeling of being held; it had been so long since anyone had touched her. She sighed happily and closed her eyes.

Adam began stroking her shoulder, and he rested his cheek on the top of her head. She could feel his warm breath blowing her hair. He felt wonderful . . . perfect. And he had the warmest hands. She smiled.

"This is wonderful," she said.

He was quiet for a long while, and when he spoke, he sounded surprised. "It is," he said.

Two little words. She couldn't imagine how he managed to put such wonder and such uncertainty in them, or such delight. His hand slid up to stroke her hair, and he sighed.

"So soft," he whispered. "And so beautiful. I never realized—" He stopped himself, and buried his face in her hair, and wrapped both arms around her . . . holding her.

His touch was wonderful; Dayne thought she could stay right where she was forever. It seemed Adam thought the same. They sat there on the couch, ignoring the movie, and the one that followed it, not talking. Just touching.

That was all. It was enough.

Hours later, Dayne said, "I'm going to have to get to bed. I work first shift tomorrow."

She looked up at him, waiting to see his reaction. He nodded. "May I see you again tomorrow?"

"I'll be off work at seven if things go well, and home shortly after that."

He nodded. "I'll call before I come over."

They walked to the door holding hands. He looked down at her and smiled awkwardly. "Good night, Dayne."

"Good night, Adam."

He turned to leave, but she tightened her grip on his hand. He turned again, and the expression on his face was puzzled.

"Could I have a good-night kiss?" She tried to ask casually, but the quaver at the end of her question said more than she'd hoped to.

He nodded, though, and turned to her . . . and she saw that his upper lip trembled. She rested a hand on his chest, and felt his heart pounding as hard as if he'd run a marathon. He moved closer and bent down, and she went up on her toes to meet him. Their lips touched, uncertainly, gently.

The kiss deepened, and Adam's arms wrapped around her and lifted her off the floor. Her legs went around his waist, her arms around his neck, her fingers twined through his hair.

The kiss went on and on, until, gasping, they pulled apart. Dayne felt as if she and the world she'd been standing on had been turned upside down. The expression on Adam's face would have been at home on the face of a man who'd just seen a miracle.

She brushed his hair off his forehead, admiring the little peak of a cowlick that curled to the right. She kissed his forehead lightly.

"That was a good-night kiss?" he asked in awed tones.

"I was impressed."

He nodded and swallowed hard. "I have to go. I'll see you tomorrow." He gently but firmly put her on the ground, and backed out the door, edgy as a cat in a thunderstorm. Dayne watched, bemused, as he all but ran down the walk across the deserted yard and jumped into his car. The motor revved to life, he jerked and sputtered out into the street, missed his gear a couple of times, then finally found it and roared away—acting, Dayne thought, very much like a man who'd never before been kissed.

She chuckled and closed the door. If that was a sample of what kissing him was going to be like, she could as easily say she'd never been kissed either.

Chapter 35

Lucifer was on the horn the instant Agonostis reached his car.

"I have never *seen* such a colossal screw-up!" he howled. He didn't sound angry, though; instead, he sounded like he was gloating. "An imp could have done a better job of getting her signature on that contract. And you can't take her another one—she isn't going to sign it after she bleeds on it."

"I've got a line on that. In the next couple of days, I'll have one of the techs draw her blood. I'll use that in the ink, and have her sign the same day. It can't miss."

"It can miss. You're almost out of time." Agonostis heard cruel amusement in Lucifer's voice. "I'm going to hang you over the Pit yet." His chuckle twisted Agonostis' bowels into a knot.

"I have time."

Lucifer was no longer laughing. He said, "I don't think so. I don't think so at all. Two more days."

Agonostis slammed on brakes, and the man who had been driving behind him—far too closely—swerved to miss him and went head-on into the rear end of someone else's parked car. Agonostis was too distressed to even enjoy that. "I have a *month*—of which I've used only four days."

"I changed my mind," Lucifer said. "I've put someone

else on the job—*but* . . . if you can bring Dayne Kuttner in by midnight Wednesday, I'll gift you with this other as a slave in Hell when I recall you—and perhaps on Earth before then, if it amuses me to do so. If you can't bring me Kuttner's soul . . . well, after I've ripped out your heart and fed it to the Pit beasts once every hour on the hour for a millennia or two, I might just make you her slave."

"*Her* who? Dayne's?"

"Jezerael's."

Agonostis' blood felt like ice in his veins. His archenemy was once again placed to take away from him everything he'd earned. "You sent Jezerael to take this job from me, too?"

"I thought she'd enjoy the opportunity. And it seemed a good idea to let her get familiar with the territory, since I have no doubt that she'll be taking your place day after tomorrow."

"But you promised me a month!" Agonostis yelled again.

"I lied," Lucifer said, and broke the connection.

Agonostis was furious—and he felt no better when he pulled into the parking lot of what had, only days before, been the abandoned warehouse. Satco was looking good; after sandblasting, the brickwork of the building was attractive, and a whole horde of imps had been put to work landscaping. He could see bits of the work by the light of pale yellow spotlights scattered among the sculpted shrubs. A discreet, elegantly lettered sign over the top of the main doors—now done up in black thermopane—read, SATCO, A TINY LITTLE DIVISION OF NETHER-LANDS INDUSTRIES.

Inside, the receptionist, a leccubus emulating female mode for the night, greeted him with a polite nod of its lovely head and murmured, "Lord and Master." He nodded and looked around the reception area. He'd stepped into deep, plush pile carpet, jade green—that was new—and a deeper green-on-green textured wallpaper, also new. The (new) reception desk was teak, and the lighting was subdued, recessed and chrome. Several chrome-and-black-leather chairs sat around a marble cube coffee table covered with upscale magazines, and potted plants sat in the corners under their own little puddles of light . . . and the whole thing looked like it had cost a bundle.

He thought of the money he'd signed for and winced. The prostitution business was pulling in big bucks, but if his underlings were going to spend money like that, he needed other sources of income right away.

He walked past the receptionist as the phone rang, and stepped through the black glass doors into the main work area. He noticed the piped-in music for the first time; he tipped his head and listened. It was an all-tuba Muzak cover of Herman's Hermits "Henry the Eighth"—which only proved that, wherever Satco was buying its furnishings, it was still getting its music straight from Hell.

He stalked past cubicles full of underlings working away on Hell's business, stepped into his office, and slammed the door behind him.

In the semi-privacy of his office, he groaned. He dropped into his chair, kicked his shoes off, and closed his eyes. Dayne's kiss still tingled on his lips, still vibrated along every trembling nerve in his entirely too human body. Her kiss . . .

It wasn't supposed to be this way, dammit. He wasn't supposed to feel anything for her—he wasn't supposed to feel *anything*. She was meat, nothing but meat.

And yet, when he closed his eyes, he could feel the silk of her hair against his cheek, and smell the scent of her, sweet and musky. He could taste her lips as they roved over his, and he could feel the tight, compact weight of her body held against him, the firm heaviness of her breasts pressed against his chest, the hard muscles of her thighs tightening against his waist—

"Enough!" he roared, and jumped to his feet. The chair rolled backward and bumped into the wall. It was his human body—the damnable human body—as full of lusts and passions as Hell was full of damned souls. His own body was bewitching him, promising him things he could never have, and could never hope for. He was damned—and if he couldn't lead her into damnation, he was worse than damned.

Still the trail of her kisses along his neck burned and seduced and enchanted. His betraying human body yearned for her. No one had warned him. No one had said, "The body has its own desires, Agonostis. The body will lead you wrong."

That was all it was, though. He took a deep breath and stood there, shaking. It was a reaction of hormones and nerve impulses, electricity and faulty human wetware. This sudden passion he felt was nothing but a chimera that would melt into nonexistence in an instant if he resumed his true form.

He stared out the glass at the Fallen working in his domain.

He couldn't think. He kept feeling, kept wanting and yearning, and his passions destroyed thought and hope of thought. The body—it was the body's fault. . . .

With a scream of anguish, he ripped away his clothing and stretched himself. He dissolved the new human body into the body of Agonostis the Fallen Angel, the second-mightiest creature ever to stride through the boiling pits of Hell. He ripped away every vestige of the human he had been and unfolded, and stretched until he was taller than the ceiling of his office would permit—until he had to smash his office door into kindling in order to walk through it. He stood up, once free of the office, and roared at his cowering slaves, puny miserling damnedsouls and underdevils, and thrilled at the collective shudder that ran through them as they prostrated themselves before him.

This was what he was. This was as it should be.

If *she* could see him now, she would cower with the rest of them—in his mind's eye, he could see her kneeling on the ground with her lovely face pressed to the floor, with her silken hair spread in a black halo on the carpet . . .

. . . with her beautiful, gentle, caring body trembling from fear of him . . .

He stopped. He stared down at his Hellish form, at his long talons and massive muscles. He thought of his face, twisted by the agonies of Hell until its onetime beauty had become a parody of itself. He didn't want her to see him this way. He didn't want her to fear him.

He wanted her to smile when she saw him coming, and to kiss him the way she'd kissed him as he was leaving. He wanted to hear her laugh, and to know that he had made her laugh; he wanted her to talk to him, he wanted her to sit beside him unspeaking, with her head on his chest.

Above all else, he wanted her to want him. In this body, his Hellish body, he still wanted those things.

Good God, he thought, what is happening to me?

Then even the phrasing of that question came clear to him, and he realized he was lost.

With luck, perhaps, Lucifer wouldn't discover the depth of his betrayal immediately. With luck, he'd have another two days with her.

Earwax appeared in a thin puff of Hell-stinking smoke. "Whoa! Big Guy—you're yourself again!" it yelped. "I'd forgotten what an ugly . . . I mean magnificent specimen of Hell you were! But hey, I just wanted to let you know—she's gone to bed now, your Evilness, so I want to go answer some phones for a while." Earwax smiled blissfully then. "Oh, man, you should have seen her in the shower tonight—when I was human, I would have paid good money to watch th— Urk!"

Agonostis grabbed the imp by his throat and dangled him in the air. "I'm going to rip your head off and eat that first," the fallen angel snarled, "or maybe I should pull your legs off and eat them, then eat your head."

The imp squeaked piteously, though it couldn't speak, because Agonostis held it by the throat.

The fallen angel brought it to his mouth and held it there, ready to bite off a leg. He didn't, though. He told himself he wasn't hungry for imp. He made the excuse that Earwax might still be useful. He gave himself half a dozen lies, and in the end, when he dropped the imp to the floor and watched it scurry away, he knew the lies for what they were.

Pity had stopped him. Pity for a stinking imp.

He was doomed.

Chapter 36

The administrator looked more like a fish than usual, Dayne thought. He stood, gaping and grinning, next to the new doctor.

"I'd like to introduce Dr. Mhya Jezick. She's collecting data for her research, and expects she'll be with you on and off for the next month. She's doing a carefully controlled double-blind study, so I'm afraid she won't be able to discuss what she's actually working on with you—that might ruin her data. But I want all of you to assist her in whatever way you can. She's to have full access to the charts and the patients . . . and your full cooperation."

"Thank you, Wynne." The new doctor rested her fingers lightly on his arm and smiled at him.

Fishface flushed.

Wynne, is it? Dayne studied the two of them. Amazingly enough, Dr. Jezick appeared to be hitting on Fishface, which seemed impossible. Why would a woman who could easily be the most perfect-looking woman on the planet have anything to do with Wynne Connelly. It couldn't be because she had any shortage of better offers.

The nursing staff nodded politely, and Fishface simpered at the new doctor. "Mhya, I've arranged a little reception for you down in the private lounge. We ought to go so you can meet your colleagues."

Mhya nodded and flashed him a blinding smile. "How thoughtful of you, Wynne."

Dayne watched the two of them turn to leave—and saw the hospital's administrator rest his hand lightly on the small of the new doctor's back. She and Mary Deiner exchanged significant glances. When the door closed, Mary shoved her notes into her pocket and made gagging noises. "What does she see in him?"

"He's hung like a Percheron?" Roxanne asked.

Mary held up a thumb and wiggled it. "Nope. I had him when he was getting his heart catheterization. Whatever his wife loves him for, it is not for his great whopping sausage."

Dayne winced. There were some things she didn't feel bore discussion, not even in the privacy of the nurses' lounge. That was one of them. She got up to leave.

"Have you ever seen anyone that gorgeous before?" Roxanne mused.

Mary said, "Oh, hell, Rox—she bought that face. The tits, too—I'd bet anything. Real people just don't look like that. And to be a *doctor* . . ." Mary laughed. "Come on . . . she's at least thirty. And she looks—what? Nineteen? Twenty?"

Dayne went out to gather her morning linen. She still had Walter "Call Me Walt" Harvey in 432-E. D was empty, though. Wilthom Fields, relieved of his gremlins, had gotten a good night's sleep and, cheerful and sane as anyone could hope to be, had transferred out to the floor for a single additional day of observation. Dr. Batskold had transferred him the night before, just before putting *himself* on an extended leave of absence and dumping his practice in the hands of Dr. Ken Weary, who, unlike Batskold, had a passing acquaintance with human beings and how to act like one.

Dayne found herself, with a touch of uncharitability, hoping Bastard didn't make it back before she left for her new job. There were some people on the planet she'd be happier never having to see again, and he was certainly high on the list.

According to Frank, there was something big going on in the ER—and if it came to the ICU, it was going to land on Dayne, since she had the only open bed. She hurried into E, hoping to get her A.M. care done before anything big came her way.

"Morning, Mr. Harvey!" She put down the fresh linens and began filling the little plastic washbasin. "How are you feeling this morning?"

"Call me Walt," he said, and laughed.

She laughed with him. "Walt, then. I forgot."

"I'm a lucky man—pacemaker just ticking away, being taken care of this morning by a lovely angel, and not a care in the world."

Dayne glanced at the third of four units of blood Walt was going to get, hanging over his head and dripping slowly into his veins, and wondered at his cheerfulness. He almost hadn't made it. According to Frank, his internist and his surgeon had both come in when he finally got up to his ICU room to discuss with him how very nearly he hadn't made it.

"He just smiled and said he'd seen the return of the age of miracles, and if he didn't live another day he would still die a happy man," Frank had reported. "He seemed to mean it."

Dayne smiled at Walt Harvey and made a joke out of his comment about angels. "No angels this morning—but at least you don't have gremlins like one of my patients yesterday."

"I *heard* about that. Frank was telling me about it. Seems one of the doctors took them all away with him—sort of like those Eskimo shamans sucking the evil spirits out of their patients."

Frank had evidently edited the story a bit. Far be it

from her to alter his version. "I suppose you could look at it that way. It was one of the best things I've ever seen that doctor do, anyway."

Walt nodded. "Quite a hero, that young fellow."

Dayne agreed with a forced smile and let the subject drop. Walt chattered on. With the blood running into him, he was perky and alert. According to Frank, he'd looked like Death when he'd finally arrived.

He rambled on, telling her about his deceased wife and about his daughters and brood of grandchildren, and she half-listened, adding appropriate comments when they occurred to her, but her heart really wasn't in it. Something Mary had said at the end of report was bothering her—something about people who were too perfect to be real.

When Roxanne said she'd never seen anyone as perfect-looking as the new Dr. Jezick, Dayne hadn't said anything. But she had seen someone precisely that perfect. In fact, he'd shown up on her doorstep the day after God released the Hellraised. Wonderful, handsome, sexy beyond words, he'd blown into town with a lot of money and no verifiable past, and had somehow gotten past her not-inconsiderable reservations; he'd worked his way, in no time, into her life and her heart.

I have this thing for trouble, she thought—this ability to pick out the men who aren't going to be good for me from any collection made up mostly of men who would. I fell once before for a handsome devil with a perfect smile. What if I have again?

She considered the other things that didn't bode well for the relationship. There weren't that many. The fact that she was expecting someone to tempt her, but that so far no one had appeared. Adam's sheer perfection. That business with the blood on the contract and the specially treated paper that burst into flames—actually, that was pretty unnerving, especially since she hadn't bothered to read the entire contract. She promised herself she would read the entire contract before she signed on with Satco. . . .

Satco? The name hadn't set off any alarms before, but it did then.

She finished the portion of Walt's morning care that he required help with and went out to chart vital signs. After she wrote down her morning assessment, she dialed information, and requested the street address listed with the phone number for Satco. She decided she'd stop by her favorite florist on the way home, get herself a few flowers, and see if whoever was there could show her how to find the place. Florists could find anything.

She thought she loved Adam D'Agonostis. She wanted to believe that he loved her. That kiss—it had been real. At least, she wanted to believe it had been real. The attraction between them wasn't just him leading her on— was it? She would have bet almost anything that he cared as much about her as she cared about him.

Was she willing to bet her soul? What if she'd signed the contract. In nursing, contracts and consent forms signed without informed consent weren't valid—so she spent a great deal of time making sure that her patients understood the meaning of each section of every piece of paper they signed. She felt almost certain that most businesses operated under the same "informed consent" restrictions.

Hell, though . . . Somehow, she didn't think Hell would be concerned about the Earthly legality of the contracts it signed. And it probably had quite a cadre of legal talent available to call on should someone raise questions. As much as anything, the fact that Adam hadn't insisted on going over the contract with her made her wonder who—and what—he really was.

The phone rang, and Roxanne got it. She handed it

over to Dayne with a grimace and said, "Emergency Room."

Dayne sighed. That would be her new admission. She got out her notepaper and said, "Hi, there. This is Dayne. Who am I talking to?"

And she took report on her new patient—he was a seven-year-old boy who'd been involved in a car accident and who hadn't been wearing his seatbelt. He'd been riding in the back seat, and the car had been involved in a slow head-on with a drunk. Mom and Dad were both fine; they'd had their seatbelts on. But the boy's diagnosis was head trauma with skull fracture and internal bleeding, and his prognosis was lousy. E.R. had just shipped him into surgery, but he was scheduled to go to Dayne when he got out of the recovery room. It was going to be a while before she got him, the E.R. nurse said, but she'd wanted Dayne to have some idea of what to expect.

Dayne hung up the phone and closed her eyes and rubbed at her temples.

A seven-year-old kid. Dayne had a hard time being objective about children. She'd been pregnant once, though she had miscarried in the sixth month. Her doctor had suggested stress as a possible reason; Dayne had just found out about another of Torry's affairs at the same time that she was working extra hours in the hospital because he was between jobs.

Her baby, a boy, had survived for a single day in the Neonatal Intensive Care unit. For one day, she had been a mother.

Torry died before they could try again. She didn't know if there would have been any other children for the two of them had he lived. Probably not; he hadn't made the best parent material in the world. But she would have thought about it, just because she'd wanted that baby so much.

This child's parents had been given a son—a perfect son—and they hadn't been careful. Such a simple precaution; a seatbelt. She couldn't help but be angry at them, even as she felt sorry for them. They'd had a responsibility, and they'd failed to live up to it.

Mary looked at her over the top of her glasses. "You okay?"

"Not really. I'm getting a little kid in, after he gets through surgery . . . if he makes it. He was in a bad auto accident."

"Oh, shit."

"Worse than that. E.R. said he was profoundly unresponsive at the scene, and he never responded to anything. Apparently he quit breathing not too long after the squad picked him up. They're having really bad internal bleeding, and increased intracranial pressure."

"That will turn him into a vegetable even if they manage to fix the internal bleeding," Mary muttered. "Once the brain swells, there isn't much hope."

"Kids are resilient," Dayne said, not believing it when she said it. "He might pull through."

Mary glanced sidelong at her and said, "You've had more than your share of miracles, don't you think?"

Dayne sighed. "Don't you wish that you could just make them better? I mean say a few words or something, and watch everything that was wrong with them just go away?"

"Of course I do. We all do. I have to ask you, Dayno— when you had your big revelation and decided to pray, why didn't you pray for something useful like that? Why in God's name did you pray for Hell on Earth? We had a gargoyle in our garden last night. It ate our neighbor's Pekes—which was fine by me, incidentally. Those damn dogs barked all night. But then it came over and rooted through my shrubs, and when I ran out to chase it off, it flew over our car and dropped a bucketload of the stinkingest . . ." Mary took a sip of her Diet Pepsi and said, "By the time we got the mess off, parts of the paint job were eaten down to the metal. And you know what my damned insurance agent told me?"

Dayne shook her head slowly.

"Insurance won't cover the damage—because gargoyles are an act of God."

"Oh, no!"

"Those weren't quite the words George used. But I was saying—you could have prayed for a sensible miracle, you know. Something that would benefit everyone." Mary flipped her chart shut and leaned back in her chair, studying Dayne. "I saw you on TV, and I heard what you said about second chances in Hell and all that—but I still think if you had thought about this, you could have asked God for a better miracle. This is the sort of miracle that's only interesting if you don't live in North Carolina."

Dr. Jezick strolled out of the break room and nodded politely to both of them. Dayne hadn't realized she was in there. The doctor put one chart back in the rack and took another, and strolled back into the break room again.

Dayne leaned over and whispered in Mary's ear, "When did she get back?"

Mary frowned and shrugged. "I didn't know she *was* back."

Dayne nodded. She had planned to watch what she said in front of the new doctor. She thought back over her conversation with Mary and decided she had said nothing she wouldn't have said had she known; but she was very glad she hadn't mentioned Adam. Somehow, it seemed important not to mention him in front of Mhya Jezick.

Dayne glance at her watch. "Oops. Mary, it's ten after.

I have some ten a.m. meds on Harvey. You have anything you want me to do for you while I'm up?"

Mary shook her head. "Thanks anyway. The next thing I have is a peritoneal dialysis at eleven. Both of mine can mostly take care of themselves."

Dayne grinned. "Nice change. Wish it was going to last."

She got up to give her meds, and suddenly found Jezick watching over her shoulder. The other woman had her hands shoved into the pockets of her lab coat. She walked surprisingly quietly in those high heels. Dayne looked her in the eye, though she had to look up quite a ways to do it; the other woman met her gaze and tipped her head to one side, while one corner of her mouth curved in an amused little smile. Jezick arched an eyebrow and waited. Dayne pursed her lips and went back to double-checking the labeling and dosage of the medications she needed to give.

She hated being watched. She really hated being watched while she gave medications; it interfered with her concentration. She didn't say anything, though. After all, the ICU staff was supposed to cooperate with the new doctor.

Chapter 37

Agonostis checked his face in the rear-view mirror. He had the human body back on—he just wished he'd paid a bit more attention to how he'd designed it the first time. When he first squeezed himself back into mortal form, he got the eyes wrong; they looked fine in the fluorescent lights of Satco, but in daylight, he saw that they were lemon yellow instead of amber. She would have noticed that. He tinkered with his shoulders and his waist and the length of his legs—the human clothing was an invaluable help in getting those details right. He just filled everything in.

But he didn't notice until he pulled into her driveway that his canines were still long and far too sharp. He was under too much stress, and he was getting sloppy.

Details, dammit, he thought. I refuse to be destroyed by mere details.

He rang the bell, and heard the sound of bare feet running across wood floors. He clenched his hands and swallowed. Even the sound of her footsteps made his heart pound and his mouth go dry. This was his last day—the last time he would ever do this.

Dayne opened the door and looked up at him; her round blue eyes could have pinned him to that spot for an eternity; for her sweet smile, he would have willingly been led astray. He wanted to scream. A day wasn't enough time. It could never be enough time.

"Hi," she said.

"Hi." His voice broke, and he cleared his throat. "I missed you."

She grinned. "Good. Come on in." She turned and walked down the hall, and he followed, wishing she were in his arms again. She told him, "I had an awful day and I'm in a terrible mood, but I'll try not to take it out on you."

"I've seen bad moods before," he told her, thinking that she couldn't imagine the sorts of bad moods he'd seen. "What made your day so awful?"

She dropped into an armchair where he couldn't sit beside her and waved him toward the couch. While he sat down, she tucked her legs under her and leaned back and sighed. "The problem this time is that I can't get a patient of mine out of my thoughts. I'm sure he was once a sweet little boy, but he isn't going to make it, and that's probably a kindness. A car accident split his skull open, and he lost one of his eyes when he went through the windshield, and asphalt scraped off half his face. He's in a coma. I don't imagine he suffered long . . . but God, it's so sad. I wish I could *do* something for him." She looked at him, watching for his reaction.

Agonostis made a face. "That's grim."

"That's work." Dayne leaned back again and closed her eyes.

"Um." Agonostis kicked his shoes off. "Anything I can do to take your mind off of it?"

She opened one eye just enough that he could tell she was looking at him. "Maybe there is. Did you bring another contract?"

He knew she was going to ask. He knew it, and he'd dreaded it. "Um . . ." he cleared his throat, and checked for spies. Not even Earwax was around right then, though

he'd been sticking to Dayne like pain on a damned soul.
He blocked Lucifer out of his mind, then extended the
block until it became a little bubble of private space that
surrounded only Dayne and himself. It wouldn't look
like much in Hell if he didn't hold it there for too long.
With luck, no one would even notice that he was hiding
something.

Then he said, "I didn't bring the contract."

Dayne's other eye opened fractionally. "No? I'm
surprised. As eager as you were to sign me up, I almost
expected you to bring another copy by last night." He
watched one eyebrow quirk upward; then she closed
both eyes again and lolled her head along the back of
her chair.

"I don't . . ." He took a deep breath. He was about
to do something he would *never* be able to explain away,
and his heart started racing again. "I don't think you
would like the company," he told her. "I exaggerated
its good points a bit—and I'm afraid the salary and
benefits wouldn't be as good as I led you to believe."

"You lied to me about the job?" Dayne sat up and
studied him. He couldn't read her expression, but the
thing he had most expected to see on her face—anger—
was notably absent.

"I . . . ah . . . misrepresented it." He sighed. "Lied.
Yes. I lied. Satco is not a company you would like."

She smiled at him then. He would have predicted
any reaction but a smile. "I . . ." She tipped her head
to one side, then rose and walked over to him and kissed
him.

He dropped his shield. Lucifer, should he chance to
spy now, would only be able to assume that things were
going well in the damnation of Dayne Kuttner. She was
climbing onto his lap, and kissing him, and unbuttoning
his shirt. He wished he understood how his failing to
get her the job he'd promised her had resulted in her

halfway undressing him. He would fail to get her a different job every day, if this was the way she took news.

He wrapped his arms around her waist and pulled her close, marveling at her body, which was both so soft and so hard.

Then she whispered in his ear, "Why don't you carry me upstairs?"

"I don't think I . . ." He clamped his shield around them for just an instant, and said, ". . . should." He had not protected her from damnation one way just to damn her another. But even as his mouth was saying he wouldn't, his body was saying he would. He wanted her. He desired her. The old line about the spirit being willing, but the flesh weak, he discovered, was based on nothing less than the truth.

Holding her tight, he stood and carried her up the stairs.

Chapter 38

"What do you mean, 'He's taking her to bed?!'"
Jezerael snarled and held a tiny brown imp off the
ground by its throat. It gurgled and gasped, but was
unable to speak. She dropped it then, and it lay on the
floor, its chest rising and falling, until she wearied of
waiting for her answer and kicked it. It bounced off
the wall and dropped to the floor a few feet away from
her and cowered there.

"Answer me, damn your eyes."

Its eyes suddenly grayed, then dried in their sockets
like raisins in the sun. "I couldn't hear all he said," the
imp screamed. "But he carried her up to her bedroom—
and when I came to you, the two of them were
undressing each other, and doing other naughty things."

"No!" Jezerael screamed. She grabbed her hair and,
enraged, ripped out two handfuls. "No!" She grabbed
up the imp and ripped it apart, then flung the pieces
around the room. "No! I will *not* spend eternity as the
slave of Agonostis."

She stormed around the office for a few moments,
then got herself under enough control that she could
plan.

"He hasn't necessarily won yet," she told herself. She
felt around for Dayne's soul, which she had tagged while
she was "working" in the ICU. Following the call of

the marker, she appeared in Dayne's apartment . . . but not in the bedroom. She didn't want to take the chance of making the situation worse, or of inadvertently doing something that might work in Agonostis' favor, instead of against him. So she was moving cautiously.

Once in the kitchen, which was disgustingly clean and cheerful, she looked up through the walls, straight into Dayne's soul. That, too, was disgustingly clean and cheerful—and completely healthy.

She frowned. If Agonostis had done his job right, Jezerael ought to have been able to see dead places in the glowing fabric of the soulstuff—she should have been able to mark a change in the overall color of the soul, too, from the gold of sunlight to a dull and angry red. But those signs of corruption simply weren't there.

She shook her head and pondered. There was no way Agonostis could think Dayne had fallen. The blind imp Jezerael had shredded could have just looked at the mortal and proclaimed her still aimed straight for Heaven.

Jezerael felt sure she was missing something. Agonostis evidently felt he was going to corrupt the girl in one vicious stroke, but he had to be laying the groundwork for that. A spiriscopic analysis would tell Jezerael what he'd done, and in which direction he'd planned the young woman's damnation.

She commandeered a spiriscope from Hell's main office. The bill came wrapped around it—it was hellish, and if it couldn't tell her anything she didn't already know, she was going to regret getting it for a very long time. She flipped the ON switch, and the puny little soul inside whined. Then she aimed it at Dayne, and line by line read the analysis of the contents of the soul of her intended victim.

When she finished, she smiled.

Not only had Agonostis failed, but in the very form

of his failure he had created a lever by which Jezerael could throw the girl straight into Hell, and Agonostis into slavery. And it was because of sheer stupidity on her archenemy's part.

Agonostis deserved what he had coming.

Chapter 39

"Oh, God . . ."

The angel at the computer terminal bit his lip and studied the screen; he twisted the plume of the pen for the Book of Names until the feather broke; then he winced. He wasn't supposed to break things. However, Dayne Kuttner and one of Hell's angels were in bed together, and the angel couldn't help but think that his trip to the water fountain was going to get him in serious trouble for negligence.

He hit the panic button.

Golden lights flashed, harp-timbered klaxons sounded, and God appeared, looking rumpled and smelling strongly of mead, glaring from a single blue eye. His Viking hat was askew and his fingers were greasy, and he had bits of food caught in his short golden beard. The giant raven on his shoulder cawed angrily at the angel, then jumped into the air and flapped slowly away.

Apparently God had been in Valhalla with the rest of the Heroes—the angel immediately regretted having to interrupt him. God always enjoyed his role as Odin, though he didn't get to play it often.

God wiped at the food in his beard and replaced the missing eye. "What's the emergency?"

The angel pointed at his computer monitor and said,

"From the looks of things, we've lost her, O Righteous and Glorious."

God studied the screen and frowned. "They're kissing."

The angel saw the frown and shivered. "Yes, sir. But they were doing quite a lot more than that a moment ago."

God raised an eyebrow, then shook his head. "What's the problem?"

"Your Holiness . . . they aren't . . . um, married. And he's one of the Fallen. And . . . well, sir, you have to admit it would look bad if she were damned."

God-as-Odin squinted hard at the monitor screen, then sighed deeply and turned to his secretary. "Of course it would look bad . . . if she were going to be damned for this. She loves him, though. There is no room for love in Hell."

"Fornication . . ."

". . . Is a sin of evil intent. No such intent exists here." God banished his spare eye and, once again pure Odin, told the angel, "Don't panic. Dayne is made of strong stuff. It would take more than a good-looking devil to lead her astray."

The angel watched him disappear, then turned back to the monitor, where Dayne and the fallen angel Agonostis still gently touched; smiling, whispering, looking into each other's eyes.

If that wasn't a sin, he thought, there were going to be one or two of Heaven's angels complaining about the fact that Hell got to send representatives to Earth but Heaven didn't. Or at least petitioning for a tour out of Christian Heaven, which had eliminated sex from its activity list. The angel, watching, thought he would be one of them.

Chapter 40

Hell's fallen angel woke weeping.

Agonostis felt the hot tears rolling down his cheeks, and jerked upright in the bed, gasping—for a moment he thought he was drowning. He wiped his eyes and caught his breath. Crying? He hadn't cried since . . .

He couldn't remember if he had ever cried, but he didn't think he had. He hadn't ever slept before, either. Neither the angels of Heaven, nor of Hell, had any need of sleep—and yet he had been as soundly asleep as any human. What did it mean?

He swung his legs over the side of the bed and stared at his reflection in Dayne's closet doors.

It means, you damned idiot, that you could have held her all night and watched her sleep, and instead you missed it. And today, everything comes to an end.

Dayne was gone—he'd known that even before he rolled over to look for her; the emptiness of the apartment around him ached like an old wound. The only sound in the place was his own breathing. The cats sat, noiseless, glaring at him from atop Dayne's dresser—cats loathed the Hellraised. He stared at them, then turned away. Everything loathed the Hellraised. Dayne would look at him the same way her cats did, if she knew what he was.

Agonostis hugged Dayne's pillow to his chest and

pressed his face into the flannel pillow case. The pillow was rich with the scent of her—hay and sunlight and some earthy shampoo. There were no such scents in Hell—he drank that one in, knowing he was losing it as surely as he would lose her. He wondered if he would even hold her again, or bury his face in her hair, or taste her lips against his, before Lucifer dragged him back into Hell. Surely the Lord of the Damned would discover Agonostis' deception before he had that chance. The Father of Lies intended to drag his one-time second-in-command back to Hell to turn him into an imp of the smallest and tastiest sort, and wasn't likely to wait until the stroke of midnight—not when he had the opportunity to change the rules yet again.

A piece of paper lay on the bed, where the pillow had been. It was a note from Dayne to him.

"Adam—I had to get to work, but you were sleeping so soundly, I hated to wake you. I'll see you this evening if you can get free from work. Love, Dayne."

She rarely got away from her job before seven P.M. He was likely to be gone before she got home—no, he was likely to be ground into component atoms and strewn about the Pit before she got home—and she would never even know what happened to him.

He could leave her a note. Something that explained his sudden, unwilling disappearance. She kept pens on her bedside table. He found one, turned her note over, and on the back started to print a quick explanation.

"Dayne—I was recalled to . . ."

He paused. Did he really want her to know what he had been? Did he really want her to hate his memory? He didn't—but suddenly he didn't want to lie to her, either.

". . . Hell. If you can, please think of me with kindness when you think of me. I'm sorry that I tried to tempt you, but pleased that you didn't fall. I will always love you. Adam D'Agonostis."

He sighed and stared at the wretch in the mirror, and wondered if she would miss him. He hoped so.

None of this had worked out the way he'd expected. He'd forgotten so much in all those millennia in Hell. He'd forgotten beauty, and the joy of silence, and the pleasure of being alone without being lonely. He'd forgotten the feel of being loved. Moreover, for the first time, he had discovered the thrill of a challenge, of being set to a nearly impossible task, with only his wits between himself and disaster. This thrill was something humans lived with daily—the opportunity to succeed or fail by their own effort. He'd tasted that opportunity in the task Lucifer had set for him, and had seen the same pleasure in Dayne's eyes when she talked about the challenges of her work—the importance of being right the first time, of thinking fast, of doing something that mattered.

She played for life, against Death—and in the brief time Agonostis had known her, he'd seen the zest she displayed for every aspect of living, because she knew from experience how thin the line was drawn between living and dying.

"God was right," Agonostis whispered. He couldn't repent—not after what God had put him through. But he could see that he'd made a mistake in supporting Lucifer's stance.

At the time, the situation had seemed so clear cut. Lucifer petitioned God for the right to give humans the knowledge they lacked. God turned down the petition, stating that humans would respect the things they earned more than the things they were given. Lucifer, incensed, played Prometheus—and in fact, most human religions still remembered his role, though imperfectly. He gave humanity the secrets of fire, and simple technology, and simple writing—and as God predicted, humanity, with no respect for its windfall, had subverted those gifts into the tools of deceit, greed, and war.

Pity he hadn't come by his wisdom millennia ago, when it could have done him some good. Now nothing but the agony of Hell's fiery Pit awaited him.

"Might as well go in to the office," he muttered to his reflection. He could completely screw up his records in just a few minutes—might as well make life miserable for Jezerael. He stood, and so did his mirror image. He cocked his head and stared at himself. He didn't look right—he'd missed something subtle.

He frowned and walked closer to the mirror, trying to figure out what was out of place. He'd gotten the look pretty close to the first incarnation of his Adam persona, but he'd made some sort of mistake in reforming himself into human shape.

"Oh, my God," he whispered. He stared at his midsection—nicely muscled, lightly furred with curling black hair that narrowed to a thin line down his lower abdomen. A thin line, unbroken by a belly button, or anything that might be mistaken for one.

"Not even a mole or a freckle there," he muttered, running his fingers across his inhumanly smooth stomach. He took a deep breath. "The bedroom was dark . . . most of the time. She couldn't have noticed."

It didn't matter. He'd lost, and he was going to end up serving Jezerael, and the fact that he'd forgotten to give himself a navel in his haste to get to Dayne would not cause so much as a blip in the currents of eternity.

He pulled on his clothes, and trudged wearily out of the apartment, carefully locking the door behind him as he left.

Chapter 41

Lucifer drummed the talons of one hand on the red lacquer of his desk, and with his other hand, twiddled the antenna of a little copper box sitting in front of him. A worried demon stood at his side, peering nervously at the speakers that still emitted only the total silence of dead air.

"I am not pleased by this, Bilgemire," Lucifer said.

"Agonostis is blocking his thoughts . . . that's all. It isn't a malfunction of the machinery. Although if there is a problem with the soul-scanner, it's Toejam's fault. She designed the main board."

"Toejam told me you did all the circuitry checks and passed this piece of trash." Lucifer glared at the little box and punched in Jezerael's code.

Immediately, Jezerael's thoughts poured out.

". . . and give the little bastard a bath in a few minutes, and when she does, I'll have her alone. Then I'll tell her she was screwed by one of Hell's angels, and that he was using her to win points with Lucifer, and that because of him, she's bound for Hell . . . <*crackle, hiss, whistle*> . . . sign the contract in a heartbeat . . . <*hiss, whine, pop*> . . . pleasure torturing Agonostis."

Lucifer smiled. At least Jezerael's thoughtbug was still functioning. He punched in Agonostis' number again, and again he got dead air—the ominous silence of something gone very, very wrong. Even when Agonostis had been blocking his thoughts, the effort it took had emitted a noisy interference that Lucifer had been able to work through with the descrambler. It was only because of the descrambler that Lucifer knew Agonostis was skimming fifteen percent of the daily take off the top of the leccubi earnings, or that he had already set up a Swiss bank account for himself.

"What time did you lose him?"

"He sort of . . . faded out at around oh-seven-hundred."

Lucifer glanced up at Hell's big clock, which showed thirteen hundred twenty-four, Hell Standard Time. "That was a very long time ago," he said in a voice grown cold and quiet. "Why didn't you call me when he began to fade?"

"I didn't think you would want to be bothered—I remembered what happened to Bootlicker. And I thought it was something that could be fixed."

Lucifer vaguely recalled Bootlicker, consigned to a thousand years as the soul in one of Hell's shovels for disturbing him at an inconvenient hour over a major matter. Lucifer loved destroying people who were actually doing their jobs when they crossed him; it kept everyone else on edge.

And here was Bilgemire, afraid to find himself sharing his doomed colleague's fate, failing to notify Lucifer of important information. The Lord of Hell smiled and leaned against his desk, looking down at the demon.

"I might as well be trying to read the thoughts of the Kuttner bitch for all this is doing," he said in conversational tones. "You've failed me, Bilgemire."

Bilgemire's warty olive green skin flushed black, and he backed up a step. He cringed and whispered, "Per-per-perhaps it isn't the technology, your Awfulness. Perhaps you've—er, *we've*, ah, lost him to the other side."

"And you didn't call me for hours after my second-in-command deserted?" Lucifer shook his head slowly, and let his smile grow bigger. "Oh, dear. What dereliction of duty that is. I'm afraid I'm going to have to demote you. One thousand years as . . . oh, what would be appropriate?" The Master of Evil rubbed his chin with an index finger and stared thoughtfully at the ceiling. "As the fuel that heats the lower reaches." Lucifer nodded. "Yes. Fully aware, constantly burning, constantly reforming. And when you've served your time, perhaps I'll permit you to work your way up to demon again . . . though I think your promotions will be slow in coming. A few millennia as an imp ought to teach you something."

The demon knelt. "Please, oh . . . please mighty Master . . . I throw myself on your mercy—"

"You missed." Lucifer flicked a finger at Bilgemire and the demon vanished with a scream.

The problem of Agonostis remained, of course. Lucifer conjured up a long-distance spiriscope and searched through the cosmic ether for his second-in-command's soul. Agonostis had always been easy to locate before—the components of his soul were scarred and twisted with rage and anger and hatred, jealousy and greed, ambition and duplicity. That raw red seething energy should have drawn the viewfinder of the spiriscope like a beacon in darkness—but Lucifer, while he found many exemplary fallen souls in the cross hairs of his lens, found none that were his missing lieutenant.

Agonostis wasn't redeemed. Lucifer would have had a message on the Hellex from God, bragging about his latest acquisition. God always sent Lucifer messages when one of the Fallen slipped out of Hell's clutches.

Lucifer frowned. Perhaps Agonostis had simply discovered the mechanism of the soul-scanner and found some ingenious method to block it. If that were the case, Lucifer wasn't going to be able to give Agonostis to Jezerael. He'd have to throw him into Research and Development instead. Set him to the task of mass-producing his invention. With several billion stealth-souls, Lucifer could stage his long-dreamed-of assault on Heaven, and God wouldn't even know Hell's army was coming until it had already overrun the place.

Lucifer nodded. That was the most likely explanation. He paged Pitchblende, and when his executive secretary arrived, told him, "I'm going to need several new demons to run the soul-scanner. I misplaced the last ones. And locate Agonostis for me. I want to know where he is and what he's doing."

Pitchblende nodded and backed out of the office. Lucifer settled into his chair and rested his hooves on his desk. He imagined the stealth-soul device, and amused himself by thinking of the fun he would have with it when it was in his possession.

Chapter 42

Dayne finished unwrapping the bandages from her seven-year-old patient's face. She was supposed to apply a new coat of Silvadene, then rewrap the head. Most of the boy's skull had been shaved before surgery, and blood had matted, black and ugly, in the remaining strands of hair.

While she did the dressing and began his bath, Dayne sang songs her mother had sung to her when she was a child.

> "If you go down to the woods tonight,
> You'd better go in disguise.
> If you go down to the woods tonight,
> You're in for a big surprise.
> 'Cause all the bears that ever were there,
> Are gonna be there again today . . .
> 'Cause today's the day the
> Teddy bears have their picnic."

She rolled him gently and applied antibiotic ointment to the abrasions on his body. He was so small, and so horribly quiet.

> "Down in the valley, the valley so low,
> Hang your head over, hear the wind blow,
> Hear the wind blow, love
> Hear the wind blow,
> Down in the valley . . ."

She started to cry. She was angry with herself—she usually managed to stay bright and cheerful and professional when she was around her patients, but her patients weren't usually seven years old. She knew the little boy's doctor was out talking with his parents right then, telling them that the life support that was keeping air in his lungs was never going to make him better, and that they ought to prepare themselves for the worst.

"It isn't fair," she whispered. She sniffled and wiped her tears from her cheeks with the sleeve of her scrub jacket.

"So few things are."

Dayne stiffened. Dr. Mhya Jezick had come in while she was singing, and had managed to do it so quietly that Dayne hadn't even suspected someone else was in the room.

"Leave, please," she told the doctor. "There is nothing here you need to see."

"No. There isn't. I've seen this sort of thing forever, it seems. It is never any more fair or right than this." The doctor smiled at Dayne, a sly smile that raised the hairs on the back of her neck. "I didn't come in here to watch you work, however. I came in here to talk to you about something very important."

Dayne went back to giving her patient a bath. "This isn't a good time. I prefer to spend my time with my patients actually paying attention to them."

"He can't hear you sing. You might as well talk to me."

"I don't know that he can't hear me. I prefer to keep in mind the possibility that he can."

"Trust me. There's nothing left of him but the body—and not an awful lot of that." Jezick didn't leave. Instead she settled into the recliner that sat next to the window, leaned back and crossed her legs.

"A group of interested persons has been watching your boyfriend."

"Adam?"

"Is that what he's calling himself? Very amusing."

"I'm not interested in hearing you bad-mouth Adam."

"You will be. Don't you think it at all strange that he appeared on the day of the Unchaining? Haven't you thought it strange that he was so charismatic, so attractive? Doesn't it seem strange to you that he managed to lure you into bed in mere days, when Dr. Prestwick tried to bed you for months and still hasn't succeeded?" She smiled. "Or that prim Dr. Weist."

Dayne put down her washcloth and dried Tad off, and put the pediatric gown on him. "I don't think Adam is any more unlikely than you."

Dr. Jezick chuckled. "Clever girl." Her smile grew broader. "Agonostis, who has apparently been calling himself Adam when he's with you, is the number one man at Satco, Lucifer's North Carolina division. He's a fallen angel—not a human, not something that ever has been human. It was his job to lead you into Hell, and he won. He betrayed you."

Dayne sighed. "And you're telling me this because you want to help me, right?"

Dr. Jezick frowned. Dayne decided her response hadn't been the one Jezick had expected.

"I assume you'll want to get even—after all, you certainly weren't one of the damned before this."

Dayne repositioned Tad, rolling him to one side and placing pillows under his upper arm and upper leg to hold him in place and keep the pressure off of his limbs. "I knew Adam was one of the Hellraised," she told Dr. Jezick. "Just as I suspected you were. I was pretty sure about Adam before I went to bed with him; I didn't have any doubt at all after." She smiled, remembering Adam's little anatomical omission—an omission that would have been just right had he been the original Adam, too.

Dr. Jezick blanched. "You . . . knew?"

"I knew. I love him, and he loves me, so I didn't feel—and still don't, for that matter—that God would hold our lovemaking against us. Not in any real, significant way. I knew Adam was trying to tempt me, too; I figured that out after the fiasco with the contract." She pulled the sheet up over Tad, and stood there resting her hand on the little boy's arm. "Adam refused to offer me the contract a second time, and told me that I wouldn't like working for Satco; when he did that, I knew he cared about me."

"He . . . did . . . *what?*" Dr. Jezick stood. "He *threw* the contest?"

"Apparently. You haven't though, have you? You're here to tempt me, too."

Mhya Jezick got out of the chair and walked to Dayne's side. She towered over Dayne, exuding the same aura of compelling sexuality and inhuman beauty that marked Adam. "Since you know why I'm here, we might as well not play games. I can give you whatever you want. You want to be rich—I can make you richer than nations. You want to be beautiful—I can make you the most stunning woman since Helen of Troy . . . who also ended up working for us, for that matter. You want power—I can make you the President of the United States, if you want the job . . . or the power behind the President, if you prefer that."

"I don't want anything."

"Of course you do. What about Agon—Adam? You want him, don't you? I can give him to you."

"He isn't yours to give." Dayne pulled a roll of tape out of her pocket and began tearing it into short, narrow strips—she needed to redress both IVs.

"He will be after today."

"No. I won't deal with you for Adam. That is in God's hands."

Mhya Jezick glared at Dayne with eyes that glowed red and evil. Then the red glow guttered out, and the fallen angel smiled. "There is something you want, after all, and if you sign my contract, consigning your soul to Hell at the end of your life, I'll give it to you."

Dayne laughed. "You're persistent, but I'm not kidding. There is nothing you can offer me that I'd even consider."

"How about the power to heal your patients?"

Dayne froze. The roll of tape dropped to the bed. Involuntarily, she glanced down at Tad—lifeless Tad, who deserved a whole life ahead of him. What if she could speak a single word and make him better? What if she could bring back his missing eye, restore his damaged face, return his wandering spirit to his body—what if she could, in an instant, give him back the life that stupidity and carelessness had stolen from him?

The ghosts of the patients she'd lost during her career paraded before her—mothers and fathers and grandparents, sisters, brothers, sons and daughters; all of them important to someone . . . all of them important to her. In the next twenty or thirty years, how many more would there be? How many more people beyond hope or help would come through those doors, begging her to do something. How many more of their families would look at her, their eyes filled with a frightening desperation, and ask, "Do you think he'll get better?"

How long would she be able to face them, if she knew that she'd had the chance to make the difference, but that she had chosen to turn it down?

Her soul, or all those lives?

She bit her lip and looked down at Tad, then up at Dr. Jezick. She was beyond words.

Dr. Jezick wasn't. She said, "I have a pen and a contract right here."

Dayne whispered, "Let me read the contract." Out of the corner of one eye, she saw a flash of blue.

Chapter 43

"I'm sorry, your Omnipotence, but I was desperate! Look!"

God, now a tall, beautiful black woman with her hair braided in cornrows, crossed her arms beneath her impressive bosom and said, "I was in the middle of blessing the crops in a drought-stricken village in Africa. I would have liked to finish."

"But she's thinking about signing!"

God gave the angel a blank stare. "Who?"

"Dayne Kuttner!"

God stopped looking put out; her mouth dropped open and she whispered, "Signing? A contract with Hell? That can't be!"

"Jezerael offered her the power to heal."

God hit a few keys on the keyboard and the scene on the monitor rewound, then ran forward. The angel once again saw Jezerael tempting Dayne, and once again heard Dayne say, "Let me read the contract."

God put the monitor on pause. "Don't watch," she said.

"What? What do you mean, don't watch."

"Even I'm tempted to interfere in this—but if we stopped her from making a decision she wished to make, we would be making a mockery of the free choice I promised humankind. So just don't watch.

Then if she signs, we won't know until we check the register."

"But Dayne Kuttner is special. She's the one who called on you to . . ."

"They're all special," God said softly, tugging on one bead-tipped braid. "I regret the mistakes each of them makes, and I hope each of them will live well. I hope Dayne will make the right choice . . . but I won't make her. She had faith in me; now I must have faith in her."

"I don't want to turn the monitor off."

God shrugged. "Then watch . . . and I'll watch with you. Remember, though, that only through the exercise of her free will can her soul grow; only through courage in the face of temptation and pain can her spirit soar."

Chapter 44

Dayne put the contract down on the bedside table. Unlike the contract that Adam had brought over, this one was short and to the point. The main clause, written in large print and plain English, specified that she would be able to do miraculous healing for her entire life—that she would be able to make the blind see, the deaf hear, the mute talk, and the lame walk. She would be able to reverse the effects of cancer, of AIDS, of madness, of massive trauma, and of the excesses of lives saturated with high-fat foods and television watching.

The second clause was very clear, too. On her death, her soul would go straight to Hell. "Do not pass GO, do not collect two hundred dollars," she muttered. The remark wasn't funny under the circumstances, but it was the first thing that came to her mind.

In the meantime, she would be able to cure anyone. She would be able to cure *everyone*, of everything.

Maybe.

She looked up at the fallen angel who was waiting for her signature with obvious eagerness. Dayne, however, was not eager to sign. It wasn't just the going to Hell, though the thought of that terrified her. She also faced the long history of stories that indicated that contracts with Hell always contained appalling loopholes geared towards making the human's sacrifice of his soul an empty one. This contract seemed too straightforward. One page. Two clauses.

The loopholes must be in the omissions.

She considered those for a moment. The first, obvious omission was how much time she would be given to work these miracles. She might drop dead immediately after signing, she realized—and then she would have sold her soul to the Devil for nothing. The more she considered that, the more likely it seemed.

"How long do I have?"

"To sign?"

"No—to live."

Jezerael frowned. "I have no way of knowing that. None of us does. Only God can foresee the future—he was very tight with that ability."

"But if I sign, you could make me drop dead immediately afterward, couldn't you? Then I wouldn't be able to heal anyone. My life wouldn't make any difference at all."

Mhya Jezick sighed. "I swear. We have an agreement with What's-His-Name that we can't hurt any of you people. Physically, anyway. So we *can't* make you drop dead, much as we might sometimes like to. You want I should stick in your contract a clause stating that you will live out your full lifespan?"

Dayne nodded. "Yes. Add that."

"Not very trusting of you." Jezick smiled again—that evil, self-satisfied smile of hers. "Lack of trust is such a good sign." The fallen angel took the contract in her hand, held it and stared at it. After a moment, she handed it back. "This is perfectly straightforward, Dayne. The contract will deliver exactly what it promises. You will be able to heal the masses. We will own your soul."

Dayne's insides twisted. If she could heal her patients, she could do so much good. How could Hell twist that into something evil?

She played out the future in her mind, imagining spending her days in doing good. She recalled the yellow stick-up notes that had covered her locker her first day back to work after the Unchaining—most of those notes had been requests for her to pray for one ailing beloved person or another. If she could not just pray for them, but actually heal them—where could the evil come from that?

Then she saw it—she saw the catch. She closed her eyes, and took one deep, steadying breath.

"Prove to me that this is something that can actually be done."

"Healing? Of course it can be done." Mhya Jezick looked annoyed. "The Bible is full of healing."

"Not by Hell's creatures." Dayne crossed her arms and looked coldly up at the fallen angel. "Prove it to me. I'm not signing away my soul for something you can't deliver."

"It's in the contract. . . ."

"And Hell is full of liars. Prove it to me. Heal him." Dayne pointed at Tad.

"*Me?* That isn't my line of work."

"I don't care. If you want my soul, you'll prove to me that this isn't something that could only be done two thousand years ago."

Mhya looked positively nonplussed. "Sign the contract and then you heal him if you want to."

"It was a fraud, then," Dayne said, and held the contract up so that she could rip it in two.

"No!" Mhya yelped. "It isn't a fraud. I just don't want to—" She studied Dayne, her head cocked slightly to one side, her eyes squinted. "You aren't going to sign until I do this, are you?"

"Not a chance."

"Oh, Hell. This is going to be a nightmare to explain to the Boss," she muttered, and reached out her hand,

and touched the child's face. He began to glow—a warm, rosy pink glow. The glow ran from Dr. Jezick's fingertips and covered the child's body like an aura. His face smoothed over, the gutted socket where his eye had been plumped out, the gouged flesh filled in. Scars erased themselves, slack muscles grew tight. . . .

And suddenly Tad thrashed in the bed. His eyes flew open, his hands wrapped around the endotracheal tube that ran from the ventilator into his mouth, and with a solid yank, he pulled it free—and began screaming at the top of his lungs, a high-pitched, childish shriek that Dayne only made out as "Moooommmmmmmmmyyyyyy!" after the third repetition. He started to rip out his IVs and Dayne managed to grab his hands and remove the needles before he could do it. She felt sure her eardrums were going to explode—her head was right next to his mouth as she worked the IV cannulas out of his skin, and that mouth never shut up.

People came running—first the other nurses, then Tad's doctor, and then Tad's parents.

There was more screaming—a lot of it. Tad ripped the bandages off his head and kicked Dayne, trying to get away; meanwhile his mother and father hugged each other and shouted incoherently at the tops of their lungs. Tad's doctor was babbling, Dayne's colleagues were shouting questions, the other alert patients on the floor began to ring their bells, demanding that someone come in and tell them what was going on—the room became a tiny point of total pandemonium.

Dayne slipped out, and Dr. Jezick followed her.

"It works," the fallen angel said.

"I see that." Dayne nodded and walked around the nurses' station; she settled into her seat and found Tad's chart. She wasn't sure how she was going to document the miraculous healing, but she thought her notes would give JCAH something to ponder when they came through, auditing charts.

"Well . . . here's the contract." Jezick pushed it towards her.

Dayne looked over at the flawless creature and shook her head. "I'm not going to sign."

Mhya Jezick paled. "What? You have to sign. We agreed."

"We didn't agree to anything. I said if you wanted my soul, you would prove to me that this wasn't something that only happened two thousand years ago. I never said I intended to give you my soul."

"You—"

"Healing seems like such a benevolent thing," Dayne interrupted. "So kind. I could make everyone better, rid the world of ills, put an end to disease." She sighed. "Except I couldn't. If I did nothing else with my every waking hour, I could heal only a few people. Who would I choose? How could I decide which people deserved to live, and which would have to die? I am only one human being. I can't make those decisions—they aren't mine to make. I do what I can to hold back death, but the right to decide between life and death belongs to God—and only God."

"Then watch that child die, and know that you could have prevented it," Jezick snarled, and pointed at the little boy on the other side of the glass wall.

Dayne shouted, "No," and reached for Jezick . . .

But nothing happened to the boy. He still clung to his mother, his arms wrapped around her neck, while she rocked him from side to side and cried into the scruffy little tufts that were left of his hair.

"Die!" Jezick pointed both hands at the child and narrowed her eyes in concentration. Again, nothing happened.

"You can't do any harm, remember?" Dayne smiled

at "Doctor" Jezick, and the fallen angel turned on her and came at her.

Adam appeared out of nothingness, right behind a bright blue monster of extraordinary ugliness who pointed at Dr. Jezick and shrieked, "There she is!"

Adam lunged at the statuesque fallen angel and tackled her. With Jezick pinned beneath him, he looked up at Dayne and yelled, "Don't sign anything! It's a trick!" Then he glared down at the ersatz doctor and growled, "I'll destroy you if you've done anything to her, Jezerael."

Dayne stood up so quickly her chair shot out behind her and slammed into the wall, then rolled into the middle of the nursing station floor again. The little blue monster jumped into it and rolled it along the floor while spinning in circles.

Dayne didn't have time to chase after the imp. Jezick/Jezerael had shifted into the true form of a fallen angel—she was easily fifteen feet tall and beautiful in the same way Dayne imagined vampires might be beautiful: seductive but deadly. She was trying to rip Adam's throat out with her teeth, all the while clawing at his face with needle-sharp talons as long as Dayne's fingers.

Adam was fighting back—but he was half the size of his opponent and lacked her dagger teeth and deadly claws.

"She can't hurt me," Dayne told herself, and jumped into the fight. She gouged at Jezerael's eyes with her thumbs, and when the enormous fallen angel let go of Adam and tried to escape, shoved a knee into her throat and braced it there.

But once she had Jezerael pinned, Dayne stopped. She hadn't been able to afford the body of a two-inch-tall dead gremlin—she hated to think how much she'd have to pay for killing off an enormous angel. Adam was safely out of Jezerael's reach, and Jezerael wasn't able to so much as touch Dayne; when she tried, her hands slid past her without making contact. It was an eerie thing to watch, but reassuring, too.

She glanced over her shoulder at Adam. "You okay?"

Adam's pale face bore the most worried expression she'd ever seen. "I'm fine. Earwax came and got me as fast as he could, but I was afraid I wouldn't get here in time. You didn't sign anything, did you?"

Earwax? Earwax got him? She decided she didn't really want to know. "I didn't sign anything, Adam."

He knelt on the blue industrial carpet, near her but not so near that Jezerael could reach him. "I'm not what you think I am."

"You're exactly what I thought you were."

"I called security," Mary Deiner yelled. "They're on their way."

Dayne couldn't imagine what Mary thought security was going to do.

Adam shook his head vehemently. "I'm *not* what you thought, though, Dayne. I'm . . . I'm what she is." He nodded at Jezerael. "I'm one of Hell's angels—just like her. Maybe even worse. After all, I've been second-in-command of Hell for eons. But I didn't want you to see me that way. And I didn't want you to go to Hell. You . . . wouldn't be happy there. And I want you to be happy."

"I'm happy with you. I knew you came from Hell, honestly I did. Well . . . not at first, but I figured it out. I love you, Adam—and it doesn't matter to me what you are. When you talked me out of joining Satco, I knew you weren't trying to damn me anymore. So it will work out for us—and as long as I can have you, I'll be happy."

He hung his head. His shoulders sagged. "You can't have me."

Dayne almost lost her grip on Jezerael. "What do you mean I can't have you? Why can't I?"

"I . . . I have to go back to Hell. I didn't do what I was supposed to do while I was here—at least not all of it. So Lucifer is going to punish me."

"He can't take you back," Dayne whispered. "I love you."

"And I love you. I'm afraid Lucifer doesn't care about such things, though. He can take me back—I knew yesterday that this was my last day. I just wanted to spend some of it with you. At least I got to see you again."

"He'll have to go through me to get you."

"I'm afraid not. And when he does get me, he will consider my love for you just another reason to punish me." Tears slid down Adam's cheeks. Dayne felt a lump forming in her throat. "Besides . . . it couldn't work for us—not for any length of time. You're one of God's children, while I am a pariah in His sight. We have no future. We cannot have a future."

"Tell God you're sorry," Dayne urged. "Don't leave me."

"I was wrong to support Lucifer—but I cannot repent; my time in Hell has made me too bitter and angry. Deep in my heart, I still blame God for the pain I have suffered." He stared at his feet. "Dayne, even if I could repent, it wouldn't matter. If I went to Heaven, I would still not be with you. You would be here, I would be there. And when you reached Heaven I would be as far below you as you will be below God. We are not equals, you and I. I'm an angel—a lesser creature. I've never faced the trials of being human."

Dayne whispered, "But I love you."

Adam smiled at her, a trembling smile that broke her heart. "Thank you. Thank you for loving me." Then he stiffened, and his gazed focused on something Dayne couldn't see.

A voice as cold and hollow as death whispered in

the air, "Agonostis . . . Jezerael—both of you have failed me. Both of you have betrayed me. Now feel my wrath."

Dayne jumped to her feet and ran to Adam, screaming, "No! Satan, you can't take him. Adam—fight him!"

She couldn't reach Adam in time; she grasped at him, but he was already shimmering, already dissolving, falling away from her into a direction and a dimension she couldn't describe, melting into the air like ice under the North Carolina sun.

"Remember me," she heard him call—his voice disembodied, its echoing hollowness a sad and empty thing.

Then he was gone.

The hospital's single day-shift security guard ran in. "Where's the emergency?"

Dayne stood in the middle of the floor, crying. Mary, hugging her and patting her on the back, told him, "You missed it, pal. We could have used some help two minutes ago."

At that moment, the little blue monster who had been sitting silently atop the nurses' station watching, decided the security guard was what it had been waiting for. It jumped at the guard, wrapped its arms around his neck, and planted a wet, slurping kiss squarely on his lips. "Hi, beautiful!" it said in a shockingly deep, radio-announcer voice, "What say you and me go someplace quiet and get to know each other re-e-e-eal good."

The man yelled and shoved the thing away from him so hard it flew into one of the glass walls facing into a patient room. The imp bounced to the floor and said, "Oh, baby, that's the way I like it." Then it ran.

The guard took off after it, billy club swinging. The ICU doors hissed shut behind the two of them, and the unit fell back into the hissing, chugging, beeping white noise that felt like silence.

Tad walked out of his room, holding hands with both of his parents. The doctor came out behind them, his face bewildered. "We're discharging Tad," he told Dayne. "I have absolutely no idea how to document a miracle . . . but I'm glad to have the opportunity to find out." He smiled ruefully.

Dayne nodded and wiped her eyes. "His chart is on the desk next to the monitors. I haven't finished my notes yet, but I'll get to them after you're done."

While he was dictating the chart, she phoned the nursing supervisor and said that she was going to be out sick for the next two days. The supervisor evidently caught some of the anguish in Dayne's voice; for the first time in Dayne's memory, she didn't try to wheedle Dayne into working the next day and "going home if you just can't manage."

Wynne Connelly, the administrator, dropped into the unit around one, a puzzled expression on his face. "Dr. Jezick had an appointment with me this afternoon," he told Dayne, trying hard to look like a man whose mind was on business. "Do you have any idea where she is?"

Dayne nodded. "She went home. I don't think there's any chance that she'll be back." Dayne nibbled the skin on the inside of her lower lip and sighed. "No chance at all, I guess."

Chapter 45

They knelt at the rim of the Pit, with the stench of sulfur and rotting flesh, and the sounds of the screams of the damned-and-undying, thick and clinging as tar around them. Agonostis, still in human form, with his human flesh blistering and blackening in the heat, crouched next to Jezerael, whose angelic flesh tolerated the Hell-furnace, even if she was not immune to the pain.

Lucifer glowered over them, slashing at them with whips, screaming incoherent threats—howling.

Agonostis could not even breathe to scream. His lungs burned and shriveled in the heat, his arms and legs pulled in to his chest as his flesh tightened and baked. He still had the power within him to change into his other, ancient form—and he knew that the pain in that form would have been less. Still horrible, still mind-breaking sooner or later—but less. But he was not the creature he had once been, and he would not don again the body of the hated thing that had once been himself. Lucifer would change him and break him. Agonostis knew that. The Archfiend would alter his body into something unspeakable, would leave him groveling and pleading for some smallest sign of mercy, and would laugh when he broke. But Agonostis held onto the thin shreds of his hard-won near-humanity; what he was suffering, Dayne would have suffered, had he tempted her into damnation. If he could never be near her again, he could find some comfort in knowing what she would have felt, and in knowing that she was safe from Lucifer's vile touch.

Lucifer caught his breath, and crouched on hands and knees in front of them, so that he could look them both in the eye. "You insufferable fuck-ups," he said in a calmer, more rational voice, "you brainless, backstabbing, incompetent Pit-meat—I'm going to hold your trials and your sentencing here, right by the side of the Pit, so that you can hear the screams of the doubly damned and think on the consequences of your betrayal while you are tried. Pitchblende!" he shrieked. "Bring me the charges."

Agonostis' vision blurred—his eyes were dry and blistering. He couldn't blink, so that he saw a steady stream of images, but the images bore little relation to what he knew was actually there. Where there had been one towering form before him, though, now he made out two.

Beside him, Jezerael screamed monotonously, already sounding very much like the Pit-buried damnedsouls she would soon join. Over her screams, Pitchblende read out the charges.

"Jezerael, once Fallen from Heaven, once mighty in our sight . . ."

Lucifer had decided to try Jezerael first; Agonostis, familiar with his procedures, knew that this meant Jezerael's charges were lesser, and that Agonostis could therefore expect his torture, when it came, to be greater.

Pitchblende read on, through Jezerael's rank and title, and droned through the charges.

"That you did willfully do good, healing to full health a child, without gaining for Hell any compensation greater than the value of said child, and that you did neglectfully fail to include such internal failsafes in the healing as would cause the child to waste away and die, in spite of external appearances of health, and that you did fail to acquire the soul of Dayne Kuttner, for which sole purpose you had been placed on Earth. How then do you plead?"

Jezerael screamed on.

"She pleads guilty, Master of Iniquity, Lord of Hatred and Pain."

"So I hear." Lucifer's voice became oily—smug and self-satisfied. "I do not tolerate incompetence or betrayal—you have been an obstacle to my will through both. This is your sentence, then. The very molecules of your body will not tolerate the presence of each other. You who have been among the highest ranked of the creatures of Hell will now be less than the lowest. You will spend a million years in the Pit as constantly burning gas, a self-aware cloud every molecule of which will feel and recognize pain. You will remember all that you have been, and all that you could have been, and you will know that you will never be such as you are again. You will have no recourse in madness, nor hiding place in loss of self. And at the end of your first punishment, you will rebuild yourself as you can, one molecule at a time, into whatever oozing, stinking form you can manage, and so you will spend the rest of eternity."

Agonostis could see the motion of Lucifer's arm— he both heard and felt the explosion beside him as the Lord of Hell vaporized Jezerael. Her screaming, horribly, didn't stop. It hung in the air, ghostly and ululating.

Lucifer chuckled; if Agonostis had had any skin left to speak of, it would have crawled.

"The charges against you are worse," he said. "The punishment will be, too."

Agonostis could hear Dayne's voice in his head, whispering *Repent! Repent!*

He would have if he could have, but one could not reach Heaven out of fear of Hell, and while the terror of what was about to become of him devoured him, he could still not abase himself before God and beg forgiveness. He could admit he was wrong—but he could not forgive God for all the things that had happened to him because he had been wrong.

Pitchblende read the charges, but Agonostis didn't listen. He heard only the sounds of the screams—only the anguish of the damnedsouls. He knew only that he would join them. So he didn't realize for an instant that Pitchblende had stopped reading, or that a third voice had intruded.

"So you charge him with loving a human, do you?" Agonostis recognized that voice. It had been more than millennia since he'd heard it—but the voice of God was not a voice any soul could ever forget.

Lucifer snarled, "My charges in my domain are my business. You have no place here."

"My place is where I choose to be, Lucifer—it has ever been thus. My business is what I say it is. And if you charge Agonostis with love of one of my children, I say my business is here."

"I'll drop that charge, then," Lucifer shouted. "I have enough others that I can sentence him to the deepest of misery for the rest of eternity."

God said, "Not so. There is no place in Hell for love. Anyone who loves truly will never be yours, Lucifer— and Agonostis loves truly."

"He doesn't love you." Agonostis could hear the sneer in the Archfiend's voice.

"No. He doesn't. But love is an emotion of hope and faith. If he does not love me now, that is of no matter. His soul is changed for the better, and may change further with time. He may come back to me someday. In the meantime, he is no longer yours."

An explosion of white light blinded Agonostis. The pain stopped, the screaming stopped, and he discovered that he could breathe again, and move his arms and legs. His knees buckled and he sobbed and fell to the ground—to a giving, spongy ground that felt like nothing he had ever touched before. His vision cleared. He was on a gray plain that was almost entirely featureless, though speckled in a few places with things of great beauty; Agonostis saw the steep banks of a rushing stream over to his right, and just a section of clear white water that rushed over huge, slick, moss-covered boulders with a delightful thunder. The stream began and ended in the nothingness of the gray plain, but the tiny section of it that existed was as lovely as anything the fallen angel had ever seen.

"This is Purgatory," God said. Agonostis looked around, but could not see God; his voice, though, was clearly audible. "Many souls find it a valuable place to work through the problems they could not deal with in life. The only things here are those things the soul creates for itself; things that have some deep significance. The creations fade after the soul has made its choice between Heaven and Hell, or has decided on one of the other options. I added Purgatory after you . . . left. You won't have seen what it can do, but its stillness and silence have been beneficial to many of my children."

Agonostis stood. He felt the peace of the place soak into him, but he did not desire such monklike peace. "Why have you brought me here, God?" he asked.

"What I told Lucifer was true. There is no place in Hell for love. But I didn't say the rest—it concerned none but the two of us. If Hell cannot hold you, Heaven cannot claim you either. There is no place in Heaven for the anger you still bear, Agonostis."

Agonostis looked around, then hung his head. "This second chance . . ." He sighed. "I don't want to appear ungrateful. I thank you with all my heart for pulling me from Lucifer's clutches."

God chuckled. "But . . . ?"

"You mentioned other options."

"There are always other options, Agonostis. They involve sacrifice, and they involve determination and courage, but there are always other options."

Agonostis swallowed, and took a deep breath. "Yes. Could I ask for one of these options? Could I return to earth?"

"To earth? I don't see how. You are neither Lucifer's angel nor mine. On earth, the powers of Hell now walk the streets in broad daylight; the powers of Heaven work, as they always have, in stillness and in subtlety. But you . . . with the forces of eternity to draw on, what power would you represent?"

"I would give up the powers of eternity."

Agonostis listened with heart tearing against his chest, while the Almighty pondered in silence.

"*Would* you?" God asked at last. "You don't know what it is to be human, Agonostis. You put on human flesh when you walked the earth, but the immortal you was still inside that flesh. You tasted both the love and the pain of human existence, but you did not taste the certain knowledge of death that drives my human children. Death is a goad, my son, the likes of which you have never known. It is the wellspring of human hope and fear, and of human creativity; all art and all science are the attempts of the human spirit to conquer it. You are a creature of eternal summer, Agonostis, and death is winter without the spring that follows. You have known many things, but you have never known grief—and if you are human, grief will shock you with its suddenness, and weigh you down with the burden of its company. It is because they can love and laugh and create beauty in the face of annihilation, knowing always that they must die, but never knowing when, that I place my human children above all the hosts of Heaven. Their courage is unlike anything you have ever experienced."

Agonostis squared his shoulders and said, "If I can be with Dayne, Almighty, I will willingly face death."

"You can take nothing with you, Agonostis, but your memories. Further, you will have a fleshly body, weak and mortal. You will have neither the powers of Hell nor the powers of Heaven—only those things that you can earn by the sweat of your brow will be yours. But you will have a human soul—and if, when you die, you are judged one of mine, you will be greater than you have ever been."

Agonostis nodded. "I understand."

God said gently, "Then go—and go with my blessing."

The gray, featureless silence of Purgatory swirled up around Agonostis, and filled his eyes and his ears and his mouth. He was filled by its emptiness, and felt himself changing, falling, growing weaker and more fragile, prey to pain and illness and huge, enveloping fear. Conversely, he felt excitement building within himself; the thrill of unimaginable adventure on the brink of happening, the wonder of a future of infinite possibility.

So this is what it is to be human, he thought.

Chapter 46

Agonostis' infernally clever plan couldn't die just because Hell had lost Agonostis, Lucifer thought. The Devil's Point theme park stood to drag in souls faster than any gimmick Hell had ever tried, but the whole concept needed to be under tough management—it needed to be in the hands of someone who was as close to irredeemable as any Hellish soul could be.

Lucifer had a few openings Earthside. Souls he had considered unsalvageable were drifting Heavenward at an alarming rate; while Hell would not be depopulated of its billions any time soon, Lucifer resented the loss of even one soul to the opposition. He needed to make sure the souls who went up to earth wouldn't keep on rising. He needed the truly hideous, the incorrigibly vile, the bitter, the viperous, the deadly—

And the worst of the lot he needed to promote Earthside as manager and place in charge of building Devil's Point.

He closed his eyes and thought, then pulled up the personnel records in Quick'N'Dead. He looked for war criminals, mass murderers, poisoners; he came up with a few possible subjects. Adolf Hitler, transmuted into his executive secretary Pitchblende, might have held some possibilities, but Lucifer considered him too tender. Pol Pot, the Cambodian nightmare, had just arrived, and would still have all the deliciously rough edges of his humanity about him, but he'd not shown any real skill at budgeting, and Lucifer wanted an operation that brought in both souls and money. Besides, he'd lacked subtlety. Genghis Khan lacked administrative skills, and was as crude as Pol Pot had been. Lucretia Borgia might have done, but she didn't work well with others. Lucifer had the same reservations about his list of serial killers. And while a few of the late American presidents had shown themselves to be both smooth liars and fine manipulators, able to work well with large numbers of people, none of the Democrats knew a damned thing about economics, and the Republicans couldn't have made a theme park fun if they'd had Walt Disney as their chief advisor—and Disney was working for the other side.

So I need to think lower profile, he thought. Someone who was a clever slime—good with money, evil as Hell itself, someone who had done horrible things and who hadn't gotten caught. He punched in the characteristics he was looking for, and waited interminably for Hell's computer system to run through its list of evildoers.

Lucifer read the printout that started churning out of the printer with some frustration. The Evilness index, which could run from a low of two hundred (high enough to get damned) to a high of one thousand, for most individuals ran in the three-fifties and four hundreds; pretty damned unimpressive. A few souls topped five hundred, but that wasn't high enough.

Just to check the numbers, Lucifer brought up Pol Pot's record. He scored in the high eight hundreds— that was very good. It was a shame he hadn't bothered to get an MBA.

But then an actual MBA popped out with a score of nine-sixty. Lucifer whistled and double-checked the records. Nine-sixty, and steady as a rock. The man's record, on the surface, was hardly a picture of evil. He'd been a small-town businessman, widowed with three kids, two boys and a girl. He'd run a tight ship business-wise, and while he was hardly well-liked in the town where he'd lived, he had managed to spend his whole life there without ever raising the suspicions of even his closest neighbors.

He'd killed his wife to get rid of her after she'd had their last child—killed her because the doctor had informed him that she wouldn't be able to have any more children. Then he'd systematically abused and molested all three of his own children. One had died in an "accident" engineered by his father when the man had suspected he was going to tell; the other two had learned their lessons and kept quiet. And when they grew up and fled, the man had started preying on children in his own neighborhood, and picking up strays. He'd gotten sicker and more deadly, until his backyard was a veritable graveyard, full of the children he'd destroyed.

No one had ever known—or if they had, they'd been too terrified to tell.

Lucifer smiled slowly and leaned back, studying the name on the paper. Nothing was lower than a child molester, a pederast, an abuser of the innocent and helpless. Not even God had much hope of seeing one of those monsters repent.

"Pitchblende!" he shouted. "Get in here! I have a job for you."

Chapter 47

Dayne, curled up on the couch, cradled the cordless phone against her shoulder and sniffled. "I don't want to be comforted, Paige. I just want to stay at home for a few days and be alone." She pulled the afghan up under her chin and said, "I'm sure. I really don't want company."

She switched off the phone and dropped it to the floor, then rolled over and shoved her face into the nubby cushions of the back of the couch. She was a lot more depressed than she'd let on to Paige—she didn't care if she never got up again. Her life felt hollow; emptier than when Torry had died, worse than when she'd lost the baby. Adam had been her hope of happiness; he'd been all her dreams rolled up into one wonderful package. He'd been her chance to get it right this time— her chance to find out if love was everything the songs and the novels said it could be.

And now, for all she knew, both of the men she'd cared for in her life were in Hell.

She wondered if she'd ever sleep again.

She clutched a throw pillow to her chest and sobbed.

"Please don't cry," a soft voice whispered in her ear. Warm lips kissed the back of her neck.

She screamed and rolled over, bringing her knees up, ready to attack whatever stranger had broken into her house—but her scream died off into silence, and her legs dropped weakly to the couch, and she gasped.

"Adam! How . . . ?" She stared at him. His face was unchanged, his body was just as she'd seen it before—except *with* navel this time. He knelt by the couch wearing nothing but the worried expression on his face, and he was the most beautiful thing she'd ever seen. Yet something about him was different. The aura of otherworldliness, the compelling air of nearly magical bad-boy sexuality—that was gone.

She was surprised to find she was glad to see it go. He seemed both more touchable and more real to her than he ever had.

She finished her question. "How are you here?"

"I made a deal with God."

"But Lucifer dragged you back to Hell."

"And God pulled me out. I loved you—and there is no love in Hell. That is, in fact, the defining characteristic of Hell."

Dayne nodded. That made sense to her. "But how did you get back here?"

"I asked God to make me human, to let me be with you."

Dayne frowned. "You were immortal."

"Now I'm something more." He wrapped his arms around her and kissed her. "I'm human. And I love you. And if you'll let me, I'll love you for the rest of my life."

"And beyond," Dayne whispered, kissing him back. "If love is the defining characteristic of Heaven, there will be a place for our love there. And I could ask for nothing more than to love you forever."

Chapter 48

God, once again in his Christian form, smiled at the scene on the monitor.

"You must be delighted to have been proven so right. This business of Hell on Earth isn't at all what I'd expected—and to have gotten another chance to redeem none less than Hell's second-in-command . . ." The recording angel leaned back from his keyboard and looked up at the Almighty.

"I'm happy for Agonostis and for Dayne. I always rejoice when my children find love, and when they triumph."

The angel chuckled. "I must say I was glad to see Jezerael get what she had coming." He looked up at God, expecting a smile, or some form of agreement. Instead, he was startled to see a tear roll down God's cheek and disappear into the luxuriant white beard. "You weren't amused?"

"No. I always hope, you see. . . . She did something good. I thought for a moment that the results of her actions might reach her—that she might feel once again the joy that comes from kindness. I always hope." The Almighty wiped at the tear, and the one that followed it. "Heaven is for you," God said gently, "and for them," as he pointed to the Earth spinning lazily below. "For me, there can be no Heaven until the last of my children is safely home."

Catch a New Rising Star of Fantasy:
☆ HOLLY LISLE ☆

"One of the hottest writers I've come across in a long time. Her entrancing characters and action-filled story will hold you spell-bound." —Mercedes Lackey